The Sound of Silence

The Sound of Silence

Anupama Samantaray Pattanaik

Translated by
Chittaranjan Pattanaik

BLACK EAGLE BOOKS
Dublin, USA | Bhubaneswar, India

 Black Eagle Books
USA address:
7464 Wisdom Lane
Dublin, OH 43016

India address:
E/312, Trident Galaxy, Kalinga Nagar,
Bhubaneswar-751003, Odisha, India

E-mail: info@blackeaglebooks.org
Website: www.blackeaglebooks.org

First International Edition Published by
Black Eagle Books, 2024

THE SOUND OF SILENCE
by **Anupama Samantaray Pattanaik**
Translated by **Chittaranjan Pattanaik**

Cover Design: **Irina Bohidar**
Interior Design: Ezy's Publication

ISBN- 978-1-64560-646-8 (Paperback)
Library of Congress Control Number: 2025931130

Printed in the United States of America

Dedicated to my grand daughter Irina and
grand son Aayaansh.

Grand Father

"The man who does not read good books is no better than the man who can not."

Mark Twain

A reader lives a thousand lives before he dies…. The man who never reads lives only one.

George R.R. Martin

CONTENTS

Translator's Note

I like my mother tongue Odia. Odia language is more than two thousand years old and recognized as a classical Language on 20th February, 2014 by the Government of India. Mrs. Anupama Pattanaik, my wife, has written hundreds of short stories and many novels in Odia. I have already translated some of her stories in the book "The new Horizen." Her stories are so unique that I could not resist but translated some of them into English and this book "The sound of silence" is a sequel to the earlier translated version. Mr. Gunter Grass said, "Translation is that which transforms everything so that nothing changes." I have tried my level best to maintain the originality of the stories. But as Paul Auster stated, "I guess the toughest things in translations are word play, which can never be reproduced exactly." However, I have made an effort to give justice to all the stories as far as possible. The need for translation arose to expose the Odia Literature to the world at Large. So that it will cross the local boundary and reach nationally and internationally. Rightly Jose Saramago commented, "writers make national literature, while translators make universal literature."

I am extremely grateful and thankful to Shri Kalandi Charan Mishra, Retd. AGM of SBI, for sincerely going through the menuscript and painfully editing it.

I like to thank my children Amit, Lory, daughter-in-Law Suchi, son-in-Law, Brijesh, grand daughter Irina and grand son Aayaansh for whom I feel this translation is necessary.

A special thanks to my grand daughter Irina who has conceptualised and designed the cover page of the book.

Last not the least, I thank the Black Eagle Publication house for publishing this book.

Chitta Ranjan Pattanaik
M: 9937542915 / 9437041915

Forward

Short story, as a popular form of literature has gained momentum since the advent of the twentieth century though it's foot prints were discernible during the nineteenth century with publication of "Annuals" by German publishers. In the long journey of story telling, possibly beginning with the Arabian nights, we have enjoyed reading great story tellers like-Anton Chekov, Guy de Maupassant, Henry James, O Henry, Somerset Maugham, to quote a few. It is true, great stories are penned in various European, latin American and oriental languages other than in English. But when the readers in general could grab a copy of the work of these none-english writers, they could comprehend the vast enormity of magnificent art of story writing. Here comes the ingenuity of the polyglot besides the versatility of the original story writers.

This collection of short stories is assiduously crafted by Ms Anupama Pattanaik on woman psychology and virtuosity, originally written in Odiya and appeared in various issues of Odiya journals. The perfect art of translation into English version by Shri Chitta Ranjan Pattanaik is manifest throughout, so much that the stories appear as if written in original English. Anupama Pattanaik has already proved herself as an accomplished story writer, highly acclaimed in the literary circle. This translated version of her short stories is an added feather in her cap. The stories verily fit into the design and shape as stated by Somerset Maugham in his book 'On literature' –"It is a piece of fiction, dealing with single incident, material or spiritual, that can be read at a sitting; it is original, it must sparkle, excite or impress, and it must have unity of effect or impression. It should move in an even line from its exposition to its close."

One of the fundamental principles of story composition is that of unity, says Hudson in his book- An introduction to the study of literature. He further states "… under which head we include unity of motive, of purpose, of action and in addition, unity of impression". Anupama Pattanaik's stories adequately fit into this principle and hence engrossing. Most of the stories revolve around women-centric plots eulogizing women's emancipation. The story 'Miser' unfolds Indrani Devi's all encompassing tacit love for the villagers. In "Repayment", the perfect depiction of an older lady's compassion and noble mode of repayment of debt by the beneficiary-the aspiring girl, is a touching tale. The issue of superstition and blind belief is deftly handled in 'Mangamma' to the reader's delight. The resilience of a devoted wife is suitably characterized in 'The Shadow' and the common trait of a devoted wife delineated magnificently.

In fine, the husband-wife duo Shri Chitta Ranjan Pattanaik and Smt. Anupama Pattanaik as translator and the story writer, have done yeoman effort to further the cause of Odiya literature and exposing them to global readers.

Kalandi Charan Mishra
Mobile - 7978487882

The Repayment

A cold night in the month of Magha. This year the winter is very severe. The temperature has dropped below twelve degrees. In the past twenty years, no one had experienced such cold. Anima pulled the blanket over her head. What is the time now? She was restless. She wished the night to pass soon. She brought the mobile kept beside her head and looked at it. It was ten minutes past one. She prayed God in her heart that anyhow the night should pass smoothly. Then let us see. She feels uncomfortable since evening and numbness in her hands and legs. At ten o' clock at night she ate a piece of bread and drank some milk and came to sleep. Son, Rajat, told time and again, "if you will feel worse, please call us. There is a calling bell switch near your bed."

Immediately after lying on the bed, pain in the left shoulder and chest started. She thought, it must have been due to gas. Only two months ago, all the checkups were done. Complete health checkup. Everything was fine. She swallowed a gelucil antacid tablet. The pain has eased a bit. She tried to sleep. But after a moment the same thing again. She took a pill again. She felt a little better for a while. But after half an hour severe pain surfaced again. Excruciating pain experienced from left side of the chest to her neck. As if somebody is loading quintal and quintals of heavy weight on her chest. Despite so much cold, she was sweating profusely. Then she thought, this must be heart attack. Otherwise, why this perspiration? The hand and legs are slowly getting numb. She could not wait more. Somehow, she pressed her hand on the calling bell switch.

By the time Anima regained her consciousness, she found her self on a hospital bed. Perhaps it was already morning. She saw her son, daughter-in-law, doctor, and nurse were standing by her bed side. All kind of tests were going on. After the doctor and nurse had left, Rajat asked, "How do you feel now."

Yes, it feels a little better, said Anima. But what happened to me? Sitting on a nearby stool, Rajat said, "At night we woke up by the sound of your bell. When we came, you were in unconscious state. We called an ambulance and brought you here. The doctor came, examined you and administered an injection. He said, it was a heart attack. If it had been ten minutes late, it would have been impossible to save your life. Another thing you might have know that a heart specialist from Delhi comes to this hospital for two days in every month. We are lucky that she has come now. She had come in the morning for an operation. She had also come and examined you thoroughly. You had also undergone x-ray, ECG and other tests. After analyzing these reports, she will tell about the next phase of treatment. Now take some rest."

At four o' clock in the afternoon, the doctor sent for Rajat. With many anxieties in his mind, Rajat entered the doctor's chamber. The doctor asked him to sit and said, "Your mother is very ill. Out of four valves of her heart one is completely and another is partially damaged. The fully damaged valve will need to be replaced and the other one will be repaired. Dr. Sunita Mohanty, the lady doctor coming from Delhi, is a specialist in valve replacement. She has gone through the entire report. Next month, during her visit, she will perform the operation. She has studied the reports for a long time and interested to do the operation herself.

Rajat was worried. Open heart surgery! How much money will be required? He has heard, how these private hospitals charge money by squeezing the patients. They are a middle-class family. Can it be possible to arrange such a large some of money? He was a little nervous and asked, approximately how much money will be spent?"

The doctor replied, "It is heart operation. Fifteen to twenty lakh rupees may be spent. However, we will discharge the patient tomorrow. We will prescribe some medicines. She should take it regularly. After twenty-one days, she will be admitted. It will take six to seven days to prepare her by doing all kind of tests. Dr. Mohanty will come and carry out the operation. You can also know about Dr. Mohanty by searching the internet. She has done many such operations and has been successful. She has a name at the international level as well."

Anima Devi was discharged and came home. Medicines were taken regularly. Now the matter is, where from so much money will come. Anima was a teacher in a privet school. Her husband had expired long time ago. She brought up her son and daughter with much difficulty. Her daughter's marriage is solemnized with a very good candidate. Son is an engineer. He is working in a privet company. He has no savings. Whatever salary he gets, is being spent. Anima got her daughter married by spending her provident fund money, she received after her retirement. The rest amounts of ten lakh rupees are kept in fixed deposit.

Anima Devi, son Rajat and daughter-in-law Rita were sitting together and talking. Rajat said, mother! There is nothing to worry about. You have a fixed deposit of ten lakh rupees. The rest, I will avail a personal loan of five lakh rupees from the bank. If still there will be a deficit, then we will mortgage the gold ornaments of the house and get the required money. Let your health get better first, then we will see. If necessary, we will sell the land in the village.

That means, all the resources of the house will be exhausted for her treatment. Anima was feeling dejected. What will happen then the condition of his son and daughter-in-law? How will they live?

Anima was thinking, "How much is the savings of a middle-class family? As the cost of health care continues to rise in these days, they are increasingly burdened with treatment costs. Their financial standards are weakening. Many middle-class families are falling below the poverty line. Then, have we no social security?"

Anima was admitted in the hospital on time. The doctors did all kinds of tests and prepared her for the operation. As per doctor's advice, Rajat made an advance deposit of four lakh rupees. Dr. Mohanty also reached from Delhi.

While taking Anima to operation theatre on a stretcher, she held the hand of Rajat tightly. She put her hands on the head of the daughter-in-Law who was standing nearby, as if she was seeing them for the last time.

Rajat could understand her sentiment and said, "Why are you bothering? Nothing will happen to you. I learnt about this lady doctor from the net. She has done many operations like this. So far none of her operations have failed. Everyone says she has magic in her hands. The patient on whom she has placed her hands, have recovered completely. But Anima's eyes were moistened. They wheeled her in to the operating room. Grief and fear contorted her face. The lady doctor came nearer wearing the surgical mask on her face. She comforted her by saying, "aunty! Are you afraid? This is a minor operation. You will recover within a few days."

Anima looked at the lady doctor's face. As she was wearing a mask, her face was not visible completely, but it seemed that her words were dripping with honey. Actually, how sweet are the words of these doctors! That reassurance made her mind somewhat firmer. After the anesthesia was given, she did not know anything.

The entire operation took almost three hours. An hour later she was taken to the ICU. After staying there for a day, she was brought to the cabin. After knowing that the operation was a complete success, Anima prayed God by joining her hands. She had to stay in the hospital for a week.

On the day of discharge, Rajat went to the bill section to pay the bill and get the clearance certificate. When the employee hand over the envelope containing the bill, Rajat wondered how much it would be. He was praying in his heart, let it be a little less. Carefully, he took out the bill from the envelope. He caught sight of the total cost. That was eighteen lakh fifty thousand rupees. While heartbroken seeing the amount of expenditure, his eyes widened in surprise. What is he seeing? There is a paid stamp in the middle of the bill. That means, the entire bill has been paid. But who had paid? Who is this well-wisher of theirs? This is utterly surprising. A cheque of four lakh rupees is attached with the bill. The four lakhs he had given as advance has also been returned. His head was reeling. He did not understand anything.

He went to the doctor and asked in a very low voice, "who is this charitable gentleman who has paid this bill?"

The doctor said, "The lady doctor who performed the operation paid the bill and she also gave this envelope to handover to your mother."

Rajat could not understand anything. Such a famous doctor, what is her relationship with his mother. When examining his mother, she did not impart any indication regarding her acquaintance with her. All this seemed to him like a puzzle. However, he took the envelope and gave it to his mother and also informed regarding payment of the bill.

Anima was also surprised and opened the envelope. She was even more surprised to see the addressing in the letter. "Mother!" Who has accepted her as mother?

She read the letter.

Mother;

Please accept my deep obeisance. You must be surprised. Kindly remember about the incident fifteen years ago. You had helped a lot to a totally unknown girl. Without your help, I could not have attended that interview in Bengaluru or achieved the position where I am today. By feeding the starving girl and spending five thousand rupees for her, you have shown your magnanimity and this is just a little repayment only. You did not give your phone number. I have tried hard to locate you. Whenever I came to Bhubaneswar, I try to find out. Always I used to think to meet you at least once. But I could not think that I will see you in such a situation. I could know you from the beginning. Even after such a long period I had recognized you. But I did not reveal my identity or elaborate the relationship. Because I have to do the operation. If the relationship is more intense, then my hands may shake. Believe me, during your heart operation, I was motionless for a moment. I was thinking, where so much mercy, forgiveness, compassion and greatness were hidden in this heart. How a heart like this could became sick?

You will recover in a few days. You just imagine that you have done a health insurance for your whole life by paying five thousand rupees. I will try to meet you when I will come to Bhubaneswar in the next month

Yours Sunita.

Anima's mind rolled back to fifteen years, to that cold morning. She boarded the prasanti express to go to Bangaluru. She had the lower berth in the three-tier air-conditioned coach. The train would leave Bhubaneswar at five thirty in the morning. In winter, it is very difficult to get up at three o' clock in the morning and go out. She had booked her known auto rikshaw from the previous night. He arrived exactly at four forty-five am. Her son wanted to drop her at the station. But she refused. Wearing a sweater and wrapping a scarf around her head, she sat in the auto rikshaw and went to the station. The train was standing on platform number one. She got up to her designated compartment and sat down. When she put her bag under the seat, she saw another bag chained and kept there. She looked up. Somebody was sleeping on the upper berth covering the entire body. Someone had come earlier than her and already slept. All the other seats were empty.

The train left on time. By that time almost all the people had occupied their seats. She leaned back on the seat and closed her eyes. Anyway, after a long period, the opportunity had come. Her niece lived with her husband in Bengaluru. There, they both had jobs. Sister Purnima had gone to her daughter's place for a few days. They had made a programme to go to Shiridi. Purnima called her over phone and asked her to come to Bengaluru and join them in Shiridi trip. For many days she had a desire to visit Baba. But she had no opportunity for it. So, when she got a chance, she took leave from the school and left.

After crossing Khurdha Road, T.T.E. came. He asked her for ticket. After verifying her ticket, he called the person on the upper berth. She must have fallen asleep. She woke up after calling for some time. Anima saw, she was a young girl. As soon as she got up, she looked around her seat frantically. Then she came down and searched. There was sign of woriness on her face. She was in tears and told the TTE, "the bag has been stolen. My money, ID card and ticket all were in it." The TTE looked at her face and said, "you were not able to know, who has stolen your hand bag within such a short time?"

The girl said, "Please believe me. I was unable to get rest for last three days due to my night duty. That is why I fell asleep as soon as I lay down on the berth. During that time somebody has taken the beg. He had not taken the beg but my future. What shall I do now? I do not see any way out."

All these words had no effect on the TTE. He said, "if you can not show the ticket, then you will have to pay the ticket price along with penalty. Otherwise, you will be forced to get down at the next station. TTE walked to the person sitting next. At that time, Anima asked the girl about her.

The girl said, "my name is Sunita. I have passed M.B.B.S. from Cuttack medical college. Now I am a house surgeon. I am going to Bengaluru to attain an interview of an American University. If I will succeed in it, then they will award me a scholarship and give me an opportunity to study there. My father is a farmer." The girl was crying.

Anima observed her as a calm and simple girl. She

studied by her hard effort and government scholarship. She became a doctor and she had a strong desire to read more. This is a golden opportunity for her. The opportunity in life comes rarely. The success in life can be achieved by prudently utilizing the opportunities.

She called the TTE and asked, "if there is any other way. Her name must be in your chart."

The TTE explained, "what if the name is in the chart? How do we know she is the same person? Her I.D. proof is required. If she will not provide her I.D. proof or PAN card then she will have to get down from the train.

The girls face seemed pitiable. Seeing her crying face, Anima decided to help her. Therefore, she asked the TTE, "How much would be the cost of ticket and fine together?"

TTE smiled and said, "only three thousand rupees." Anima took out the money she had kept for Sai Baba wrapped in a piece of red cloth and handed over three thousand rupees to the TTE.

The girl stared in surprise.
Anima said, "why are you looking like this? Keep the receipt. You will definitely attain the interview and be successful. This is my blessing. A mother's blessing."

Sunita touched her feet and cried. She was relieved, as such a great danger has been averted.

Anima asked for breakfast for Sunita. When the pantry man came to take order for lunch, she asked Sunita whether she would eat veg or non-veg.

Sunita stared blankly.

Anima said, "will you attain the interview in empty stomach? I am ordering a chicken mill for you.

Sunita shook her head in affirmative. Even she forced her to eat dinner. When asked who is in Bengaluru to help her, she replied, "there will be no problem once I reach there. A senior girl is working there. I will stay with her. Her younger brother will come to the station to pick me up."

After a long time, the train reached Bengaluru city station. Anima put two thousand rupees in her hand said, "Keep it. You may need it."

Sunita could not believe that such a person could exist in this world. Her eyes became moist with tears.

Anima said, "You will return it with interest after becoming a great doctor."

After getting off from the train, everybody took their own destination. Sunita touched her feet and left with the boy who came to pick her up. Sunita requested for her phone number but Anita said, "We will meet automatically if there is luck."

The husband of her niece came to take Anima. On the appointed day they went to Shiridi. She could not pay the money, she had kept for Sai Baba. Prostrating there, she prayed, I have spent it for a noble cause. I will pay it later.

The girl of that day has become an eminent lady doctor during this time. And look at the coincidence, such a critical operation was performed by her hands. Not only that, she also borne the expenses of a large amount. She had helped her a little from the humanitarian point of view. But she returned the principal with cumulative interest. As the saying goes, "if you will give four annas, you will receive back twelve annas." This has happened similarly. Who says the world has changed. There is no religion, no honesty at all. But she knows that if you do something good for someone with an open heart, you will get back everything with interest.

Since then, she tried to go to Shiridi once again but could not go or could not pay five thousand rupees.

But now she will go definitely after her recovery. Saying everything to her son, she joined her hands in reverence to Sai Baba.

The son and daughter-in-law stared at her face with astonishment and tried to measure the depth of her heart.

***

"There is no duty more obligatory than the repayment of kindness." - Marcus Tullius Circero

The Unique Wife

No one can tell when, where, at what moment the course of human life will take a turn. A simple, beautiful life can suddenly be battered by a ferocious tsunami or a stormy life can suddenly became a beautiful, calm and sweet life. When faced with a critical situation, man cannot turn back but rather, by making new efforts from that situation, he may be able to change the future outcome.

Anindita was thinking about the course of events that had taken a new turn in her life. So many thoughts were circulating in her mind. What will she do now? what can she do?

Anindita was sitting on the balcony of her gorgeous bungalow. Her gaze was stretched towards western sky. The colourful glow of the setting sun did not make her happy but rather disturbed her mind. The reddish sun will set now. It will be complete dark. The sun knows that he will rise again, heralding the arrival of a new dawn, spreading its light. The whole earth will glitter in that light. But she? There is no possibility of light again in the deep darkness that is engulfing her life.

Someone's evil eye is cast on her. Why did the unseasonal storm blast into her life. Her passage was spread with thorns. She had considered herself lucky. She was born in an ordinary middle-class family. After getting a good proposal, her father did not let it go out of his hand. He got her married. Her marriage was solemnized only five years back. She felt blessed to have a husband like Arindam. Arindam is truly an exception. She had no idea that such good person could exist in this world. Such a great engineer, job in a big company, fat salary, car, bungalow but there is no ego at all. Rather he is very calm, polite and gentle. He is always eager to help his friends and relatives in their bad times. He has fulfilled all her hopes and desires. Even in his busy schedule, he takes her for outings.

A few days back, they went to Shimla to celebrate their fifth marriage anniversary with their two-year-old daughter. They had booked a hotel for three days. There, one day she felt very weak suddenly. She had a slight fever but the desire to eat decreased substantially. They did not pay much attention to it, thinking it might be a fever due to cold.

Even after returning from Shimla, the fever persisted. It did not subside even after taking medicine. There was no appetite at all. As per doctor's advice, the blood test was conducted and the result was terrible. She had blood cancer and the disease was in advance stage. The white blood cells were dying. Have to give chemo quickly. But there is little hope of improvement. Anindita could hear it when the doctor said this to Arindam.

What is this? The afternoon of the life arrived before the arrival of noon. As if her chest was bursting with severe pain. How old is she ? Few days back her thirtieth birthday was passed. How can someone leaves the world so soon? But what is in her hand? Everything is the will of the ruler of the universe.

She is not afraid of dying. No worries for Arindam either. He is only thirty-five-year-old. Due to his qualifications and social status, he can be happily married for the second time. But what will happen to their daughter,

Anamika? She is only two years old child. What will she do? Who will take care of her? Can Arindam look after her properly? If her step mother abuses her after marriage, then her life will become hell. Oh! She cannot think more. What is solution to this problem? Only deep darkness before her eyes. But light has to be found out from the darkness. Something has to be done. She cannot leave her daughter so helpless.

Arindam is sitting in his office. A lot of works remains pending. Many days passed due to their outside trip and Anindita's sickness. He was not able to concentrate on work since last two months. Still, he does not feel like working. He was very much worried. The doctor's cruel truth was pounding in his ears- "Blood cancer, less hope." That means … oh … cannot think anymore. Nothing like that was known before. But how the disease has spread so far? Anindita never complains anything. She tolerates everything without any grumble till the things become critical. Leave it, let it happen …What is in man's hand? Treatment is going on. She is being treated at home as per the doctor's advice. Every now and then the doctor visits the house to see the patient. A maid is engaged for cooking and also to look after her. Everything is on track. Now he must be determined and stick to his work. Meanwhile his friend Dinesh had made two rounds. Dinesh has a separate chamber in his office. When he came again, Arindam thought, he must have some work with him but could not tell it. Therefore, he called him and asked, "What happened is there anything to do?"

There was a mysterious smile on Dinesh's face. He smiled softly and said, "What else do we have to do? All the works are yours."

What do you mean? Arindam stared in surprise at

his words. He called Dinesh and asked him to sit on a chair in front him, ordered two cups of coffee through the peon. Then he asked him, "What is the matter?"

Dinesh said without any preliminary, "Do you want to marry a second time?"

Arindam laughed a little and said with surprise, "why are you saying this? I have neither a fight with your sister-in-law nor I divorced her. Why should I think of such an absurd thing?"

Dinesh had the same smile on his face. He extended a piece of newspaper to Arindam and said, "See this and you will know whether I am telling the truth or lie."

Arindam took the newspaper from his hand and looked at it. So far, he had taken the matter lightly. Thought it was a joke. Now he is really worried. He read the advertisement again, - "A thirty-five years old young man, who is an engineer and has a well-paid job in a reputed company, requires a beautiful, educated and cultured girl. Interested persons can contact on the mobile number given below."

Even though his name was not mentioned in it, he understood that the advertisement was written keeping him in mind. Because it was the mobile number of Anindita and Dinesh knew that number. That is why he was so dramatic. Arindam took the newspaper from him.

Dinesh spoke, "Now I am going to my chamber. But please inquire and tell me what is the matter."

Holding the paper, Arindam was sitting as before. He did not feel like working anymore. What is this madness of Anindita? Has the illness of the body infected the head? Did she lose her mental balance? He did not notice any such abnormality with her. But for the physical health, the strength of mind is essential.

Arindam returned from the office little early. As he reached home, Anindita asked, "You had said, it would be a little late. But you came early. Are you feeling ok?"

Arindam looked at Anindita. The beautiful figure of Anindita has become miserable. Black patches under the eyes. The hairs of the head are falling due to the effect of chemo therapy. The body is gradually getting weakened. His mind became restless. He dragged a chair and sat near her – he touched gently her head and said, "What is all this, Nanda?"

Anindita looked at him questioningly. He handed over the piece of newspaper to her and said, "is it correct to advertise like this without my knowledge? Will not the people make fun of me?"

Anindita said in a calm voice, "would you have agreed if you had been told? My days are running out. Two months have passed quickly. How many more days will I live? I have to think about your future as well as daughter's future. After knowing that your future is secured, I can die peacefully."

Arindam put his hand on her mouth and said, "do not speak like this, Nanda! You will be all right."

A sorrowful smile played on Anindita's lips. No matter how much the medical science advances, this disease is not so easy to be cured. For that, keeping your future in sight, I have prepared the plan.

Plan! what plan? Arindam stared in amazement.

Anindita explained, "I will talk to the girls in appropriate time, who have contacted me after seeing this advertisement. I will explain everything to them clearly. I will choose a beautiful, sober girl among those who have agreed to the proposal, of course, with your advice and consent. After my demise that girl will marry you and take all the responsibilities of Anamika. During this period, she has to come and stay here. So that Anamika will completely get acquainted with her. As a result, she will not have any problem in future."

Pressing hands on his ears, Arindham told in a slight loud voice, "Please stop all these things. No one will agree to such a proposal. Apart from it, I do not want this. I can never think of a second marriage."

Anindita said in her usual calm voice, "everything is done only when necessary. There is a saying, "necessity is the mother of invention." It is a common thing that when a woman dies, the man marries again and bring home a wife. This is not a new thing. Of course, our matter is a little different. I am thinking of your marriage while I am still alive and I want to bring your future wife to our home. Look! You have a long unending road ahead of you. You cannot walk that path alone. You need a partner. This is my desire. Consider it as the last wish of a dying person. The person going to be hanged is also asked about his last wish and attempts are made to fulfil it. Would not you fulfil my last wish? I request you, please agree. Then I can die in peace."

Arindam embraced her and started crying. Tears also flowed from Anindita's eyes. The flow of Ganga, Jamuna from the eyes of these two people removed their sadness, frustration, depression and disappointment for a while.

After a week, Anindita received a lot of calls on her mobile. Some of the calls are directly from the girls and some are from the parents of the girls. She asked everyone to send their bio data in her address or email it. Now is the computer age. Most of the bio datas came to her email. Only two have come by post. She read them all with interest and decided to call six of them. She showed the photos to Arindam and sought his opinion.

Arindham has made up his mind since that day that he will not disagree with Anindita in any matter. He will not bother her with any complaints or objections. He said, "You do whatever feels right to you."

Anindita called them one after another to talk on holidays, Saturdays or Sundays. That too in the presence of Arindam.

Most of the girls or their parents did not agree to the proposal after hearing everything. Why would a person give his daughter in marriage to a married man? Further the diseased wife is alive. There is also a daughter. Some called her crazy.

Two girls had agreed to the proposal. One came wearing a torn jean pant and banian. She said, "I have no problem. I will hire a nanny to take care of the girl. However, it will be better if the marriage will take place sooner."

The other one was very ultra-modern. The girl dressed in palazzo and Punjabi, sat in front of her in such a way that, Anindita felt as if she was being interviewed by that girl. After hearing everything from Anindita, the girl said, "You should have mentioned all these things thoroughly in your advertisement." However, she agreed to the proposal and explained the reasons - "She wants to live a luxurious life and for that money is required. Here, her future husband is in a high position. So, there will be no problem."

Anindita was upset. The eyes of all these people are only on wealth and money. They are so selfish and narrow minded. How will they handle her daughter and husband?

Anindita's mind was filled with sadness. The hope for the success of her plan was slowly diminishing. However, she did not despair. She has to think something else. Meanwhile she should not be heartbroken. After thinking a lot, an idea struck to her mind.

While going to sleep at night, she said to Arindham, "You divorce me."

"What nonsense! Do you know what you are talking about?" Arindam retorted.

Anindita insisted in her usual calm voice, "Hey! What is there to be angry about. I am telling this after much thought. The girls from the good families do not agree because you have a married wife. But after divorce many fathers will agree to get their daughters marry you."

Arindam was furious and said, "what is this madness? How can I think that I will divorce you at this time? What will the people say? leave that matter. As you are my spouse, the cost of your treatment amounting lakhs of rupees is reimbursed by the company. This facility will not available after the divorce."

But Anindita persisted stubbornly. She pleaded, "I do not need any treatment. I would have died tomorrow but will die today. But before that I will settle your and Anamika's future."

Arindam was stunned. He understood that Anindita was speaking with all seriousness. After thinking a while, he said, "all right. But please wait another week. If any other girl will not send her profile to you or we will not achieve any success within this time then only we will take a decision."

After two days, a phone call came. As usual she told her to send the biodata.

That also came through registered post. As per Anindita's direction father, mother and daughter reached at their house at 10 o'clock on a Sunday.

Anindita asked them to sit down and watched for a while. A very normal family. Probably lower middle class. Casually dressed. The green synthetic saree on daughter

Abantika looked very good. Even if it was s cheap saree, it suited her very much. Abantika is not so beautiful but she is not repulsive. Anindita told them the whole story and also briefed Abantika what to do. Arindam was sitting quietly near her.

After hearing everything, Abantika's father Rajesh babu said, "Look! we respect your feelings. How a woman, whatever she may be, arranges her husband's marriage is beyond our imagination. Truly a better half like you is rare. You are unique. We did not know that much. Please give us some time. We will let you know after discussing among ourselves."

Anindita was impressed by their behaviour and conversation. It seemed to her that this girl was the perfect candidate. She did not want to lose her. Therefore, she told them, "Look! I have very little time. I would feel a little comfortable if you would declare your decision today. If you want, you can sit and discuss in our another room. The lunch will be prepared here."

Rajesh babu seemed like a very good gentle man. The white hair on his head with white pant and shirt accentuated his personality. Even though he was dressed in the most ordinary clothes, still he was recognisable among many people. Abantika's mother did not say anything, but seemed like a prudent housewife from a middle-class family.

Rajesh babu said, "all right. But it will take two or three hours. This is not a small matter. It is the matter of our daughter's whole life. But our daughter is outstanding in every field."

The room was shown to them. They had discussed inside the room. The cook gave them three cups of tea.

They came out after two and half hours. Lunch was

already ready. At the request of Anindita and Arindam they took their Lunch. After the eating was over, Rajesh babu started talking, "See! we are from a lower middle-class family. This daughter of mine has passed B.A. We do not have the required capacity to marry off our daughter to such a highly educated and high salaried person. Your sacrificing attitude has impressed us a lot. When you desire to put another person in your place and take your last breath in peace, we are ready to co-operate with you in that noble work. You can trust Abantika. She can make your hopes and dreams come true." Anindita was very happy."

Suddenly Abantika said, "I have something to speak."

Everyone stared in rapt attention. Abantika continued, "if the marriage will be materialised here, I do not need any child in future. I have only one daughter, Anamika. I cannot give birth to another child and make anyone else to share her love."

Anindita looked at Abantika with wide eyes and astonishment. It took some time to understand the exact meaning of Abantika's statement. Then she got up, embraced her and cried. These tears are not of remorse but of joy and happiness of finding something unexpected.

Arindam looked at Anindita. Her health has decreased considerably. But she is searching a wife for him without thinking about herself or worrying for herself. Trying to make his future life happy. Ah! How much pain she must have felt. Oh God! Why did you punish her like this? His eyes became moist.

Looking at the sorrowful face of him, Anindita said, "You are sitting completely silent. Please say something. Need to know your opinion too."

Arindam said with a little smile, "I know that whatever you do, you will do it for my welfare and for our family. So, what else do I have to say? Your happiness is also my happiness. He got up from there and wiped his eyes stealthily."

Anyway, it is finally settled that after two days, Abantika will come and stay in this house. Anindita was happy. In this way, Arindam and Abantika can understand each other better. Anamika will get acquainted well with her new mother. After her death, they will marry and start their marital life.

Rajesh babu said, "All these are fine. But there should be an agreement between us. Then my daughter's future will be safe."

That was done. Everything was written in detail on the stamp paper and every one signed it. Anindita thought, a new era has begun.

Two days later, Abantika came to stay at home. Anindita happily welcomed her. What needs to be done, she explained her everything in detail. Abantika was able to take control of all the household chores within five days. She was doing effortlessly and smoothly all the works like giving food, tiffin to Arindam at his office time, all works of Anamika i.e. eating, bathing, dressing and also feeding Anindita with proper food on time, giving medicine etc. How beautifully she is doing. Anyway, she was thanking herself that the selection of candidate was perfect.

Abantika was doing all the works of every one properly. She was also doing all the works of Anindita, even though she had a nurse for her. She was instructing the nurse to do everything rightly. Very soon she bound Anamika with her love and affection. Anindita taught her daughter to call Abantika as new mama. Now she is running after Abantika, calling her new mama, new mama. Now a days Arindam is always looking for Abantika for everything. Sometimes Anindita felt jealousy in her mind. This is the inborn nature of every woman. But she restrains herself from it. She has done all these herself for the well-being of her daughter. To make Arindam happy. How painful it is to sacrifice your partner in the hands of another person. But what can be done? What else will you say to anyone when your luck had failed you. Is Arindam really inclining towards Abantika? So, what is the harm? After some days they will lead a family life as husband and wife.

The time is flying. The time of Anindita's departure from this world is drawing near. Now it is not so painful. Anamika has completely accepted the new mama. She is even sleeping with her. Arindam also seems very happy. Sometimes he takes Abantika outside. Everyone is happy. Now she can breathe her last in peace. The treatment is going on in full swing. Abantika is taking full care of Anindita like a younger sister.

Anindita is feeling a little better than before. The hair lost during the chemo therapy has grown back. The dark slots under the eyes have gradually disappeared. Ten months have passed since then. As per the doctor's advice, she will have a check-up. A blood sample was given for testing purpose. Arindam took her to the doctor. The doctor did a lot of tests and experiments. Also saw the blood test reports. Both are looking at the doctor's face. What will come out of his mouth, will determine the future of their family. The doctor looked at Anindita's face. Then he revealed, "It turned out to be a miracle. There is nothing to fear or worry about. Madam is now fully recovered. Only she has to come in between for check up and take some medicines regularly. She can now lead a normal life."

No one was prepared for this unexpected happiness. For a while both of them were speechless. Then Arindam's face lit up. "However, his efforts were not in vain." He thought. Overjoyed, he looked at Anindita. What is this? why is this shadow of sadness on Anindita's face? Can she not believe it? Getting rid of such a dreaded disease despite the doctor's adverse remarks, is not a small matter.

On the way back, Arindam expressed, "You have heard such a wonderful thing but there is no joy on your face."

Anindita responded, "returning from the jaws of death is definitely a happy matter. But all the plans are depending on my death. In the current situation, everything has turned upside down. What will happen to Abantika now? How will we break her hope and faith in which she is staying here."

He said with a smile, "It is not so big a deal. There is nothing to worry about. She is in the prime of her life. She is not unattractive to look at. She is also educated. She can marry somewhere and start a family."

But after staying here for so long, people must have seen her differently. How will she get rid of it?

Hearing Anindita's concern, Arindam said, "You do not think about it. All will be well."

It will be all right! How easily Arindam is saying. A girl staying in their house for so long with much expectation and doing everything smoothly and efficiently. She will be thrown away today. She cannot be so selfish. She cannot deceive her, cannot thwart her hope. Whatever it may be, she will fulfil all her hopes and dreams.

As soon as they reached home, Arindam told loudly to Abantika, "Hey! Cook good food. Feeling very hungry."

But Anindita was worried after observing Abantika's face. What is it? Why does she look so pale? The face is completely withered. Does she know something? No ... No

… how it will happen? She asked her, "Why do you look so pale?"

Leave it. Please tell me what the doctor said.

Anindita thought, "Probably she is too eager to start her marital life."

Before Anindita could say anything, Arindam said, "What else he will say. She is fully recovered. Nothing to worry."

Really! Abantika's face lit up with happiness. She divulged, "you know didi ! when you went to see the doctor, I kept fasting even without taking a drop of water wishing for your welfare. Anyhow, God heard my prayer."

Anindita looked at Abantika. What a loving and simple girl. She fasts and pray God for her cure. But what she was pondering. She has to do something for the happy life of Abantika. After thinking a lot, a definite plan came to her mind.

While going to sleep at night, she told Arindam, "I have no more attraction in this world. After taking initiation from a guru, I will become an ascetic (sanyasini). I will spend rest of my life in the services of God, who has given me a new lease of life. You live happily with Abantika."

Arindam said with a little smile, "You see Nanda! No body becomes a sanyasi or sanyasini by mearly saying. For that separate environment, penance and time are required. Your time has not come yet. So, leave the idea of being a sanyasini. Eat right, sleep right. Take care of your body. Try to live happily. Other things will be taken care of later."

Next day, Abantika's father, Rajesh babu had arrived. He wanted to take his daughter to his home for a few days. There was no objection from anyone to this. Abantika put some clothes in a bag and about to leave. Holding Anindita, she cried a lot. Anindita said, "come back soon.

Your presence is highly required here. The responsibilities of Anamika is in your hands."

After paying obeisance, she left.

After the departure of Abantika, the house seemed empty. Within these few days, she had managed the house pretty well. Anamika also searched a lot for her new mama.

Arindam said, "It has been a long time since you have gone for an outing. Let us go somewhere. You will feel good. Yes! Why go anywhere else. A drama is being performed at Janata Theatre. Let us go to see that play."

But Anindita did not agree. She said, "I do not like any dramatic performance. I will stay at home and think about our future activities."

There is no need to worry. Stay relaxed. After watching the play, we will think something together. Arindam forced her to agree.

The play will start at 7 P.M. Arindam & Anindita got ready to go. They also prepared Anamika.

They met Rajesh babu at the entrance gate of the theatre hall. The same white hair, white dress. Probably he always wears white dresses like this. Every person has different likings. Anyway, Anindita greeted him and enquired, "You have also come to see the play. What about Abantika?"

"Yes, she has also come. She is inside." Replied Rajesh babu.

The theatre hall was full. There was no vacant seat left. They went forward and sat down in the front row.

A popular novel of a famous novelist will be played. Renowned actress Sanghamitra will act in it.

The play started on time. However, Anindita could not see anything clearly. Thousands of thoughts were playing in her mind. How to solve their problems. She could not find any solution. Sometimes it happens. Even if you are looking at it, you can not see what is in front of your eyes. Due to the extreme worriness of the mind, the brain is not able to accept the pictures of events in front of your eyes. Anindita was exactly in that state. Even though she was looking at the stage, she could not understand or know anything.

Anindita came to senses when suddenly Anamika shouted, "new mama, new mama." She stared at the stage intently. Hey! It is true. The heroine looks exactly like Abantika. She shook and asked Arindam, "Does not she look like our Abantika?"

Arindam said in a low voice, "She is not like Abantika but she herself is Abantika."

"What do you mean? What is she doing here?" She asked in surprise.

There are a lot of things to say. I will tell you later. Now you watch quietly.

Not later. Tell me now. What is all this? I do not understand anything. There was anxiety in Anindita's voice.

Arindam understood that Anindita was very much worried. He said without giving her any further agony, "I was thinking to say it later but now I am disclosing it. Please listen."

Arindam began in a quiet tone, "When you were interviewing the girls after advertising in the newspapers, but none of the girls were selected, then I was very happy that this madness of yours will not succeed. I do not know why but I consulted a psychologist. He counselled, if you get what you want and the satisfaction and happiness derived out of it may be the successful treatment of your disease. Because the mental state of the patient plays a big role in the treatment. An idea came to my mind and I contacted the authorities of this Janata theatre for its successful implementation. After much pleading, they arranged for me to meet their best actress. I have told everything to Sanghamitra and requested her to help and co-operate with me to help a dying woman either to die peacefully or for her recovery. Further I also told her, "I cannot pay the price for it but I will pay double the amount of your fees as long as you stay at my home and act."

She is a very good-natured girl. She responded, "I will act in this situation. If by that one finds peace or gets rid of serious illness, then that will be my greatest reward. Money is not my purpose. But I will take as much as I need to run my house. After that Sanghamitra came as Abantika and two of her theatre party artists came as her father and mother.

Anindita was staring at Arindam with bewildered eyes. Arindam has done so much! So much efforts to cure her! It was his unrequited love for her that brought her back from the brink of death. And Abantika! She acted very well. Totally flawless performance.

The curtain fell on the drama. Every one stood up and started to leave. Anindita ran to the green room.

Tired Sanghamitra was sitting on a chair with her eyes closed. Anindita went and embraced her. Tears were rolling down with emotion. How great you are! Apart from this stage performance, how flawlessly you performed in my house. I am really grateful to you. Meanwhile the manager and other artists of Janata theatre had reached there. The manager announced, "this is the pinnacle of the art of a true actress. Sanghamitra has been nominated for the best actress of the year award for her long acting without any stage, without dialogue and also without direction."

Sanghamitra politely folded her hands and said, "I was just acting. But I accepted you as my elder sister. Gradually a pleasant bond grew in me for you. I was always praying for your speedy recovery. However, you are fully cured. I cannot tell how much happy I am."

Arindam breathed a sigh of relief. He was happy for the success of his plan.

Anamika could not understand anything in her small head. She was only dragging Abantika (Sanghamitra), "New mama, let us go."

Somehow, they explained her and returned home. While returning, Anindita was thinking, "how many things happened in her life. She never thought that the spring will come with all its grandeur, the sweet voice of cuckoo will be heard in her life again. Everything is in the hands of the ruler of the universe."

Involuntarily she bowed down before Almighty.

***

"If you live to be a hundred, I want to live to be a hundred minus one day. So I never have to live without you."- A. A. Milne

The Self Respect

Today the village is humming with activities from the morning. There is a ripple of happiness spreading in the atmosphere. Starting from children to the grown-ups there is a flow of joy in every one's body and mind. Everyone is calling each other and going towards village pond. At home, the women are busy in grinding the spices. Some are grinding in the modern grinders but some are also grinding on the old stone slabs. Whereas some are using onion, garlic and ginger, others are using mustard seeds. One does not need a precious thing for his happiness. Happiness can be derived from small things or events. The reason for the happiness in the village today is that after long ten years the fishes will be caught from the village pond. The fishes must have grown quite large. Every household in the village will be given their share. The rest will be sold and deposited in the village fund.

There is only one pond in the village. But it is quite large in size. It is full of water throughout the year. Because there is a big spring on the west side of the pond. Water always flows out of that spring. In the result water regularly comes out of the pond by the eastern side drain and the water in the pond remain clear all the time. But since two years, perhaps a big part of the spring has been buried in the sediment. The water is not coming out as before. The pond water is getting polluted due to non-discharge of water. That is why the Panchayat has sanctioned some money at the request of villagers. In this money, the pond water will be drained and the sediments will be removed. Around fifty members of the youth organisation are ready to remove the sediments. They have refused to engage any machine for the removal of the mud. They have demanded that the youth organisation would clean the sediment and take money for it. They will build a house for the youth organisation with that money. The villagers had also agreed to this

All three water pumps are running. The noise of people and the sound of running pumps creates an atmosphere of festival. After the water in the pond dried up about more than half, the fishing started. As the water level was getting low and due to dragging of nets in the pond, the fishes stared jumping. The joy and curiosity of the children on the pond's embankment was increasing. Plenty of fishes were caught. After the catching of fishes, the water were pumped again. In a short time the water in the pond dried up completely. Only the mud remained. This time, it was the turn of the young men of the organization. They all put on half pants and put a piece of polythine inside their baskets and went out to remove the mud.

Some people have already brought bullock carts to carry the mud. Mud is a good fertilizer. If used, it will increase the fertility of the land. However, the mud cleaning operation of the pond went on in full swing.

There is a deepadandi (A raised Temple Like structure) exactly in the middle of the pond. Gradually the boys reached near the deepadandi. Ten to twelve boys took out the mud by their spades and fill it in the baskets. Ramesh is using his spade rapidly. He is scraping the mud from the vicinity of deepadandi and filling it in the baskets. Suddenly he felt something different object come into contact with his spade. He kept aside his spade and searched the lump of mud. Something was wrapped in a polythene packet. The other boys also came to him with interest when they saw him stop working suddenly. Ramesh opened it after cleaning the mud from the polythene packet. There was something wrapped in a piece of cloth.

What could be inside ? It was a packet wrapped in so many layers. With great excitement, he opened the cloth packet. What is this? Everybody was surprised. There were a pair of gold bangles inside the cloth packet. The news of the discovery of gold bangles in the pond spread like lightning in the village. As soon as he heard it, Harihar Mardaraj, the richest man in the village and the former Land Lord (Jjamindar), came to the bank of the pond. He saw that a pair of gold bangles were kept on a square white cloth. His eyes widened. Those are the same bangles. His ancestor's royal bracelets. The bangles are fitted with precious stones and filled with various artistic works. The bangles which were stolen almost one year ago, is now kept in front of his eyes. Even the people of the village had already known whose bangles they were. When they saw Harihar, everyone said, sir! Your bangles have been found.

After thanking the boys of the youth Association and promising to give them some money in the form of donation, Harihar returned home with the pair of bangles.

How was it possible? How many incidents had happened over the years in connection with the theft of these bangles. What was the meaning of hiding those in the mud. Harihar's head was getting heavy. He remembered the day when the bangles were lost. How angry he was. It was normal to get angry. They are the ancestral bangles. Who dared to steel it from the house in broad day light?

His family consists of two sons and a daughter. The daughter is already married. Elder son Dhirendra is a

Lecturer. Younger son Narendra still continuing his study in college. Dhirendra fell in love with a girl. She was from a lower middle class family. But got good education. She has done her post graduation in science. Also took B.Ed. training. But Harihar did not agree at all to accept that girl as his daughter-in-law. Dhirendra was very stubborn to marry that girl only. At last Harihar agreed. Because, he was afraid of the children of these days and also both of them are educated and adult. If they will marry of their own, then he cannot do anything. Even he cannot deprive them from his properties. So he gave his consent and got them married on an auspicious day.

Arundhati came home as daughter-in-law. Her father has given her gifts as per his capacity. But those were too little for the standard of Harihar's family. However, as per the tradition of the house, the mother-in-law made her daughter-in-law wear these ancestral gold bangles on her wrists. The old fashioned artwork on the thick gold bangles and the red coloured valuable gem stones fitted on it looked very beautiful.

After Astamangala (eighth day after marriage) Arundhati's brother came with some necessary things. Next day he left early in the morning. After the departure of his brother, Arundhati went to bathe. She removed the bangles from her hands and placed them on the dressing table. When she came back after bathing, she did not find any bangle. Although she fully remembered that she had placed those on the dressing table, still she searched the dressing table drawers. But there was no sign of bangles. Then she could realise that the bangles were stolen. Who stole those in such a little time during day time? She immediately informed it to Dhirendra.

As soon as he heard this news, there was an explosion

in the house. Harihar was in absolute anger and told what ever came to his mind. The bangles were ancestral jewels of many generations. They were stolen from the house in board day light. Who dared it.

Generally people have an impression that the poor people have no morality. Getting a chance, they can do any dirty work for money. The mentality of Harihar was the same. His first suspicion was on Radha, the maid of the house. But she has been working in their house since ten years. Until today, no adverse traits of her have been observed by any one. Still he called her and asked her regarding the theft. Even threatened her in the name of police. But Radha had only one answer, "she did not do it". She vehemently said that she did not go to Arundhati's room on that day. So there was no opportunity to take the bangles. However, Harihar could not accept her arguement. Suddenly an idea struck to his mind. Arun, the brother of Arundhati, had come with some articles for his sister and he had gone in the early morning. Has he taken the pair of bangles with him? The more he thought it, the stronger his feeling became. He already had a grudge against Arundhati and her family for this marriage. This incident seemed to supply him more fuel. Gradually his suspicion began to seem true to him. He also called all his family members and apprised them about his suspicion. Further he said that, "he wants to give a chance to Arun. He will send a man to the paternal house of Arundhati. If he will not return the bangles, then he will take the help of police."

Arundhati opposed vehemently. She said, "We may be poor but not a thief or cheat. Our education and culture will not permit us to do it. My brother, Arun, can not do such a work ever. Apart from it, I kept the bangles on the dressing table and went to bathroom only after my brother left the house.

But Harihar did not give any importance to her version. He told directly to his daughter-in-law that, "you have given those bangles to your brother. By selling it, there may be some improvement in their financial condition."

As if the chest of Arundhati was bursting with grief and humiliation, she could not say anything. Only tears were pouring from her eyes. Dhirendra also stood silently, not saying anything. Stealing of bangles and father's anger made him helpless.

Harihar sent a man on motorcycle to Arundhati's village. He had sent a letter to his Samudi (Father-in-law of his son) through him. That was not a letter but a threatening order, -"return the bangles or face the consequences."

At first, Arundhati's father Abhiram babu did not understand anything. He called Arun and inquired.

Arun said, "You have made us such humans by giving us culture and education, so that we can not do such things even if we die."

But Abhiram babu was worried. It is not a good sign for a new relationship. Who knows, how is the mental condition of Arundhati? Thinking all these matters, he said to Arun, "take out the motorcycle. All these doubts must be cleared by going there immediately.

Arun also came out instantly. The distance between two villages is only fifteen kilometers. In no time they reached their house. Seeing them Harihara's anger rose in a flash. He abused them like anything. All the anger, resentment, hatred and bitterness that had been accumulated in his mind came out like the red hot Lava of a volcano.

Arun could not tolerate all these things. His body trembled in anger. He also responded in a loud voice, "uncle! check your tongue. We may be poorer than you but we have our own dignity and self respect. All these words do not sound good in your mouth. If you will tell anything more, I have the power and ability to retort."

Harihar fell silent. But immediately he started to the police station and reported the gold theft matter. He also mentioned his suspicion on Arun and Radha. The police also soon became active and summoned both of them to the police station. Radha's house was searched. But nothing was found. Arun was interrogated and their house at village was searched too. The same thing, nothing was recovered. Finally, the police released both of them after taking undertakings.

Every action has a reaction. This action of Harihar had elicited far-reaching reactions. Radha left the village. Once a maid comes under the circle of suspicion, she does not easily find work in other people's homes. Therefore, she had to leave the village.

After a month of this incident, Abhiram babu died of heart attack. Perhaps, he could not bear this insult. It was beyond his capacity to avenge this humiliation. Calm, simple, innocent people cannot do anything when they get hurt. But like, "salt eats the pot, worry eats the body," the flames of the insult are always smoldering in their minds. Smoldering like this one day they will be burnt to ashes.

It is better not to talk about Arundhati. No one treated her in right perspective. Dhirendra also seemed to accept the views of his father. He never opposed or protested his father's words of portraying Arun as a thief. He only consoled Arundhati that "everything will be fine."

Arundhati's mind was filled with sorrow. What else will be right? If one could call the brother of his daughter-in-law a thief, then there arose a question of trust. The faith with which she had come to Dhirendra's house, Dhirendra could not keep it or did not even try to keep it. Her mind was filled with despair. At this time, the death of her father hit her hard. She could not endure this blow. She had gone to her father's purification rites but never returned to her mother-in-law's house. Surprisingly, Harihar and even Dhirendra did not show any interest to bring her back. She also made up her mind not to return.

After the death of Abhiram babu, the condition of his house became miserable. Mental trauma coupled with financial crisis made their situation even more unbearable. Arundhati made her mind strong. She has to do something. Her brother is studying. His studies must continue. Many of her college friends have got jobs and well established. She made contact with some of them and applied for jobs to different places. She had the qualifications. So, she got a job immediately in a renowned private school. That too in capital Bhubaneswar. Immediately, she sent her brother to the hostel and came to Bhubaneswar with her mother. A new chapter began in her life.

XXXXX

Dhirendra came and saw the bangles. The square piece of white cloth wrapped the bangles rather than the bangles aroused more interest in his mind. He observed that piece of cloth for a long time.

Harihar was surprised and became angry. He retorted, "why are you looking to that peace of cloth so minutely. Think about whose work was this? Who took the bangles and threw those in to the pond? What was his purpose?

Dhirendra said in a slow tone, "Father! I already knew whose work is this. After a while you will also know it. He sent for Narendra. Narendra had come to the village for the fishing purpose.

Narendra came and stood before them and asked "have you called me?"

Dhirendra shook his head and went towards him and suddenly slapped him on the cheek. He asked "tell me, why did you do such a thing?"

Narendra said hesitantly, "I do not know anything about this."

Dhirendra said in a slightly strong voice, "do not know! whether you recognise this piece of cloth or not. Remember, at the time of my marriage, I brought one set i.e. six numbers of these branded handkerchiefs. And you selected this cream coloured handkerchief from them. Look here, the name of the branded company is written on this cloth. The pair of bangles were wrapped in this handkerchief.

As if, Harihar fell from the sky. Angrily, he turned towards Narendra. Dhirendra restrained him with great difficulty.

Harihar said, "This theft case still exists in the police file. Police will come and investigate, who threw these bangles in the pond. Tell all the truth. Then you can be saved by requesting police. Otherwise you will go to jail definitely.

Narendra was scared and told all the truth. He said that, on the fateful day he intended to wake up early in the morning to see Arun, as he was scheduled to leave in the morning. By the time he woke up, it was too late. So, he hurriedly went to his sister-in-law's room. But no one was there. His eyes fell on the bangles kept on the dressing table. Sometimes, people do such things that they never thought, they could do it. It is like the devil enters his head. That was his condition. Meanwhile, he fell in love with a girl who always wanted expensive gifts. She desired to eat in good hotels, buy gorgeous sarees and dresses. In the process of fulfilling the wishes of that girl, he borrowed a lot of money.

As the Land Lord's son, he was getting things on credit from the market. But he will have to pay it. So, seeing the bangles, he could not resist the temptation. Without delay, without thinking anything, he took the pair of bangles.

There must be an uproar after the bangles were found stolen. After the situation calms down a bit, he will sell them to meet his needs. But for the present they have to be kept somewhere. After thinking a lot, an idea came to his mind. He wrapped those bangles in the handkerchief, tied it well in knots and kept it in a thick polythene bag and fastened its month. He again tied the face of the polythene bag with a long thick thread. Hiding it in his lungi, he went to the pond to take bath. Reaching the pond, he went to the bottom of the dipadandi under water and saw a small hole there. He put the polythene bag inside the hole and tied the other end of the thick thread to the cast iron hook attached to the dipadandi. The depth of water near the dipadandi will be about seven to eight feet. He hoped that in such depth, no one would be able to detect it. In a few days, he planned to take out the bangles from there and sell them. But the situation became so complicated that, he could not dare to take it out anymore. Meanwhile, perhaps a fish or an aquatic animal had cut the thick thread and the polythene bag was buried in the mud.

Hearing Narendra's confession, Harihar and Dhirendra were stunned. No one had dreamed that Narendra would have done this.

What did you do? Because of you, two families were destroyed. Your brother's married life was ruined. An innocent man's life was lost in heart attack. A poor, despondent woman left the village. Harihar's throat choked in pain.

Making his voice as soft possible, he said, Narendra must be punished for the mistake he has done. But first the daughter-in-law has to be brought back. The poor fellow was punished without any fault of her.

The very next day, Harihar, his wife Kanakalata and Dhirendra went to Bhubaneswar to bring back Arundhati. By that time, Arundhati also came to know regarding the bangles. Hearing the door bell, Arundhati opened the door and was astonished seeing her mother-in-law, father-in-law and husband in front of her. Her heart was filled with anger and humiliation. However, making herself as normal as possible, she bowed down to them and called them in.

Without any preamble, Harihar said, "something had gone wrong, daughter! Now let us go home. Dhirendra also said, we have made a mistake. Now we know who the real thief was. Whatever happened has already happened. Now come home with us."

Kanakalata held the hands of her daughter-in-law and pleaded, "forget the past. Manythings happen like this in a family life. You can not manage, if you will take these things seriously. We all have come running to take you back. Do not dishearten us".

All these soft and pleasant words did not make any impact on Arundhati's mind. Rather; her body was burning with anger. She could not bear it anymore. She retorted, "what do you think you are? In the abundance of wealth you are forgetting that we are also human beings. Even if we are poor, we have respect in the society. We have nothing except self-respect and you have tarnished it by making false accusations. As the truth has come out to light to day, you have come running to take me back. Through out ages, women have been oppressed and exploited. Shriram, the noble man of Ramayana, also made the same mistake. After conquering Lanka and rescuing Sita, she had to under go a fire test (Agni Parikhya) to prove her chastity and after coming to Ayodhya, Shriram sent her to the forest at the rumors spread by his subjects. When mother Sita finally returned to Ayodhya with her Sons Laba and Kusha, She was again asked to undergo the fire test.

Mother Sita was deeply hurt. That insult was unbearable. Finally she prayed to mother earth "O' mother! I can not take this anymore. Please give me shelter in your lap" Seeing her suffering the earth split in to two parts and Sita entered in to it. No matter how hard the all powerful Rama Chandra tried, no matter how much he prayed, she did not hear anything. She was absorbed in the lap of mother earth for ever.

All these facts may not be unknown to you still I told it. Because in the pride of wealth you may have forgotten that every women has self respect and self dignity. She is not a toy so that you can make her dance to your tunes. A woman can tolerate everything but can not bear injustice.

Then she looked at Dhirendra and said, "the faith with which I went to your house, the promise you had made on the marriage alter at the time of making seven rounds to protect your wife, that faith and that promise have been broken by you. I do not need any more help. I can live alone. I have already taken this decision."

Harihar was surprised at Anuradha's long speech. He could not imagine that the girl who looks calm and simple could be fiery like a volcano. He thought that she would be happy and come back with them. Dhirendra also expected that. But No……. she will stay with her self-respect. Nothing more need be said.

***

"Self-respect is the fruit of discipline, the sense of dignity grows with the ability to say no to oneself." - Abraham Joshua Heschel

The Divorce

The month of Asadha was coming to an end. It had been drizzling since four days. No chance of going on a morning Walk. It is a different kind of pleasure to sleep in a wet and cold morning. But today the weather is a little better. Although Sujit had no intent but he went out for a morning walk. As usual, he walked on that particular route. The rectangular ground inside the press colony has a black top road around it. Both sides of the road are full of the trees like Roseberry, pine, Neem etc. Now after the rain, the trees are clear, greener and dense. He started walking speedily, with the hope of meeting any of his friends. But no. No one is in sight. When one turns the corner of the rectangular road, the movement of the people can be seen on the front road. Due to thick trees and vines nothing else could be seen.

Just as he turned north, he saw Mrs. Das walking about sixty feet away. Perhaps the wind was flowing from that side and the fragrance of her perfume was coming a little bit. Mrs. Das's husband, major Das, was martyred last year in Kashmir, fighting with the terrorists. Their only daughter is studying engineering outside. Mrs Das has almost reached the corner of the road. Just then, the unfortunate incident happened. From nowhere two youths came speeding on a black motor cycle and stopped near Mrs Das. The boy sitting on the pillion came jumping, flashed a knife and pulled the gold chain from Mrs. Das's neck. As soon as he sat on the motorcycle, the driver rushed forward. All these happened within twenty to thirty seconds. Sujit saw the motorcycle is racing towards him very fast. Mrs. Das was shouting while waving her hands. Without caring anything the two youths are rushing ahead. Even though they saw him, they probably did not care about his presence. Sujit has a walking stick of two feet three inches in his hand. At the top of the stick there is a spherical object made of brass. Sujit had no time to think anything else. The motorcycle was approaching very fast. As soon as it came closer, Sujit grabbed the bottom of the stick and hit hard on the helmeted face of the motorcycle driver. Perhaps they were not prepared for it. So the driver's hand automatically went up to protect his face. As the hands lifted from the handle of the motorcycle, the motorcycle lost control and crashed in to a nearby electric pole. The two boys were hurled away.

Meanwhile, some morning walkers came running. Someone must have called the police. Immediately Sujit took some photos in his mobile. Some people went and grabbed the two boys. Good luck. As they fell on the bush, they had no serious injury except slight scratches. About ten minutes later police had arrived. The gold chain was recovered from the pocket of a boy. After hearing everything, the police arrested both of them and took them to the police station. Statements of Mrs. Das, Sujit, and two others were also taken.

After departure of the police, Sujit was examining the broken walking stick. He purchased it from the last handicraft exhibition. He did not realize that Mrs. Das was standing there.

Mrs. Das said, "Thank you very much, sir. I got back the chain only for you. Further, the wicked boys also received the punishment".

This was the first interaction of Sujit with Mrs. Das. Not that, they have not met before. But the conversation never happened.

Sujit has retired two years ago. His son and daughter are both married and staying outside. He and his wife Sarika are residing at their home in Bhubaneswar. It is his habit since long to go for morning walk every day. Now a days he meets Mrs. Das during the morning walk. Her residence is in the next street. After this incident, they usually talk a little whenever they meet. As the days passed by, friendship developed between them. Some of his friends have started joking. The outlook of these people is such that only the negative things are seen by them. There are many relationships between women and men. But they cannot understand. Only one relationship is visible to them.

He tries to explain, "In this ripe age there is no warmth or emotion. The mind is steady. Just like the calm water of a pond, not like the unfettered waves of the sea". Again he made them understand that, a lonely widow requires three protections i.e. social, economical and mental. The financial state of Mrs. Das is fully secured. Mentally also she is very strong. Therefore, we have a duty to provide her social security. So, we need to keep in touch with her and call her to our puja committee as a member of our colony development Association. She has to be made aware that she is a part of this society and also an adorable personality of this community.

But there are some people in our society who will see worms in a fresh fish. They cannot bear the happiness of others, but feels a sadistic pleasure in making them sad. Exactly that has happened. A colorful picture of Sujit and Mrs. Das's relationship has reached at wife Sarika. Sujit had gone to market. After returning, Mahabharata started in their home. As if Sarika was waiting for his return like a hunter waiting for his prey. Her whole body was shaking with anger. She said whatever came to her month, "Oh! The romance has started. Shame on you, to act like this at this age."

Sujit tried to explain in a clam voice, look! Someone must have poisoned your mind. Otherwise, do not you know your husband? Further at this age when the entire body became cold, there is no excitement left now.

But Sarika refused to listen anything. She retorted, "How will you believe these husbands. What are you telling me about age? You know the story of a retired major here in Bhubaneswar who killed his wife and cut the body into three hundred pieces to be thrown in different places. It was due to his newfound love with a lady. Look! Stop morning walk from tomorrow. No matter where you stumble upon Mrs. Das do not talk with her. Otherwise I will go to my parent's house.

Sarika's house is in Bhubaneswar. She has three stout brothers. They love her very much as she is there only sister. That is why Sarika is so proud. In the eyes of a woman, her father is the best man in the world, the most beautiful woman is her mother and she herself is the most intelligent person. But her own husband is incompetent, miser, selfish, Lier, Stupid. Sujit felt that there was no use in explaining anything to Sarika. His morning walk was stopped.

Anyway, the days passed well. But one day a telephone call came from the police station, to identify the two people who tried to snatch the gold chain, in the identification parade. Mrs Das telephoned. She is also going to the police station in her car. She requested Sujit to accompany her. Sujit left the house saying that he had received a call from the police station.

By the time the work at the police station was over, it was already evening. On their return, Mrs Das requested Sujit to have a cup of tea at her residence and unable to avoid her request Sujit entered the house. After about half an hour he came back to his house.

When he came home, he observed that the situation was out of control. The news of Sujit going in the car with Mrs. Das had reached Sarika. So, Sarika was sitting in the house of Parida Babu which is situated in front of Mrs. Das's house. In the evening, when she saw them getting down from the car and entering the house while talking, her anger rose to the top. She came home and waited for Sujit to return.

When danger comes, it comes with friends and relatives. When Sujit was returning from Mrs Das's house, Mrs. Das got up from the nearby chair and followed him to the gate to see him off. She lunged forward as her legs entangled with a fallen internet cable. As a result, her face hit Sujit's back. This is a trivial matter. But Sujit's white shirt was stained with the light lipstick mark of Mrs. Das's lip. And unfortunately it fell on Sarika's eyes first.

Sarika said, as far as possible, in a calm voice even though she was trembling in anger, "I cannot stay here to see your love affair. Immediately I am going to my parents' house." Then she called an auto rickshaw and arranged her clothes in a trolley bag. No matter how much Sujit tried to explain, she refuse to listen. As soon as the auto rickshaw came, she took her bag and left. Only thing she told at the time of leaving, "soon you will get the divorce notice from me".

Sujit stood motionless. He knew the stubbornness of Sarika. So it is not impossible on her part to send a divorce notice. He also got a little angry. How can she take such a harsh decision for such a petty matter? How can she think of leaving him at this age and staying at her parent's house? Now what he will do after son, daughter-in- law, daughter, son-in- law, friends and relatives come to know this matter? Everyone will blame him. What will he do now? His head was in turmoil. Will he consult with his friends? No….. No…..Nothing will be done by them. Rather the matter will be disclosed. Suddenly he remembered his daughter. Daughter Ragini is living in Mumbai with her husband. Ragini is an engineer and intelligent also. He phoned and told her everything from the beginning to the end.

After hearing everything, Ragini reassured him and said, "Do not worry at all. I am doing something."

Sujit was relieved. He took rest on the bed. After some time he fell asleep. Early in the morning his sleep was broken. Still he was lying as before. What to do? There is no chance of going in morning walk. He got up late and finish his daily routines. He made some tea and drank it. The house seems empty and lonely. What will he do? Will he call Sarika? No……No…… as she is angry, she will tell so many things. Did she tell all these there? Oh God! In what situation I dragged myself? He did not go out of the house. He cooked and ate whatever was available. Day passed and night descended. However, there was no phone call from his daughter. The night also passed in a state of worriness and anxiety. Hearing the calling bell sound at around 8 o' clock in the morning, he opened the door and greatly surprised. What is he seeing. Sarika herself is standing with her brother. He was scared a little. But the brother-in-law greeted him and said, "I have some work. I am going". Sarika also entered the house without saying anything and started arranging all the things speedily. Sujit stared blankly without understanding anything. Then he switched on the TV and sat down.

After some time Sarika came to him and said "why are you sitting? Go and bring necessary things from the market. You must bring meat. Our daughter is coming in this twelve o' clock flight."

Sujit could understand the meaning of this miracle. Their daughter must be up to something. He started for the market with light mood. He has to go to the airport also.

Ragini arrived on time. Her five-year-old daughter was with her. Her face had a serious expression. Sarika touched gently Ragini's head and body and said, "Why do you look so pale? You came alone but son-in-law did not come."

Ragini responded, "Leave those things. First give me something to eat". Sarika served the food. After eating Ragini announced, "I will not go their again. I have come here to stay forever".

As if Sarika's head was spinning. Worriedly see looked at the face of Ragini with questing eyes.

The gist of what Ragini said was, "Four days ago Rajesh, her husband, had a party. The boys and girls drank and danced until midnight. One girl had drunk so much that she was almost out of sense. Everybody had gone to their respective homes. But Rajesh brought that girl to our house. Further, the next day, he himself took her in his car and left her at her home. All the troubles are for that."

Sarika caressed the head of her daughter and consoled, "Look baby! If you are leading a family life then you have to endure all the difficulties in the life. There are many storms, Cyclones, Incidents and accidents occur in a worldly life. For that why does one ruin her own family life and runaway like this?" Then she said to Sujit, "Hey! Please elucidate our daughter. Talk to Rajesh on phone."

As usual Sujit told impassively, "It is good. You go

and stay in your parents' house and our daughter will stay in her parents' house."

Sarika said in a tense voice, "Please do not tell like that. This is about the life of our dear daughter. What face will we have before our friends, relatives and neighbours? Perhaps one wrong decision of mine has brought such a storm in my daughter's life. It is said that the children are being punished for the mistakes done by their parents.

Sujit spoke, "See! Do not look negatively in everything you see. Every matter has its positive side. Anyway, do not worry. I will talk to Rajesh."

He dialled Rajesh.

From the other end Rajesh divulged, "After hearing everything from Ragini, this was our plan. She has gone to her home. Let her stay for seven to eight days. Then I will go and bring her back."

After departure of Ragini, the house felt a little empty. Sarika was not fully normal yet. The topic of Mrs. Das was not discussed at all. The morning walk of Sujit was also stopped. He was thinking to bring a treadmill and install it on the rooftop. The days were passing well.

Rakhi Purnima arrived. Like every year, Sarika wanted to go home to tie Rakhi around the wrists of her brothers. So both of them went there in the morning, had lunch and came back at 4 o' clock. Sarika changed her clothes and went to make tea. Hearing the calling bell, Sujit opened the door. He was stunned to see Mrs. Das. He was visualising danger in his mind. But he kept the thoughts in his mind and invited her inside, offered a seat and called Sarika, "Hey look! Who has come".

Sarika's face turned pale when she saw Mrs. Das. Meanwhile, Mrs. Das took out a rakhi and sweet packet from her bag. She said, "Sister-in-law! I had come in the morning but your house was locked." She tied the Rakhi around the wrist of Sujit and fed him a sweet. She again told to Sarika "you know sister-in-law, brother has helped me a lot." The hardness of Sarika's face was gradually softening.

As Mrs. Das was about to leave, Srika held her hands and made her sit down. She said, you have come to our home for the first time. Would not you like a cup of tea? However, I was going to make tea for us just now.

Although Mrs. Das refused, Sarika went and brought tea, biscuits.

After tea party was over, she went inside and brought a carry bag. She handed over it to Mrs. Das and said, "It is on behalf of your brother (Bhaina)."

"What is this?" saying this, Mrs. Das brought out the object from the carry bag and saw it was a saree. What is this sister-in-law? What is the necessity of all these things? I know that after tying the rakhi, the brother has to give something to his sister. But, what is the need of all this at this advance age? Brother must have brought the saree for you. It will look good on you. Please, keep this saree for you. Your help and cooperation are enough for me. I am going now.

Sarika went to the gate to see off Mrs. Das. Sujit was standing at the door. His head, which had been heavy for so long, Became lighter. Sarika was giving Mrs. Das that laced purple coloured saree that he had brought for her last month for eight thousand rupees. That means, Sarika has no ill feeling in her mind.

His eyes became moist with happiness.

***

"Now a days Love is a matter of chance, matrimony a matter of money and divorce a matter of course." - Helen Row Land

The Mother Mangamma

Sunday has a different feeling. The body and mind feel sluggish. There is no intent to get up early in the morning. Perhaps that is because there is no daily routine work. Everything is done according to one's own will. Archana was tossing and turning on the bed even though she had been awakened since a long time. She thought that she would take rest all the day. Even she will not cook but order food from outside. Only two people are in the house. Still, there is no escape from the work. Devendra joined in a private company after retirement. So it is usual work as before. Now he has gone for a morning walk. After his arrival, she will get up and make tea. She clutched the pillow and lay down for a while. The sun rays have fallen inside the house through the windows. It is past seven. Still she does not want to get up. Suddenly the mobile rang. She got annoyed. This mobile is disturbing at any time. She picked up the mobile and saw that the call is from her son Manoj. She sat up quickly. There is no time to make a phone call during busy schedule. They have calls only during Saturdays and Sundays. But so early in the morning…

She switched on the phone.

Manoj's voice from the other end, "Mama! I have mailed something to you. Please open your e-mail and read. Then we will talk."

Archana smiled a little. This is the age of e-mail. Previously letters were sent through Post Office. It was not known when it would be delivered. Sometimes it took more than fifteen days. Now it takes less than a minute to send a letter by e-mail. What an e-era! Everything is done by it, like-epayment, e-deposit, e-ticket, e-transfer, e-conference etc. etc. But Manoj never mailed before. Usually, they talk on the phone or on skype. He mailed for the first time. What could be the reason? Eagerly she opened the mail.

She read the mail in one breath. What she understood was that Manoj's son had some skin problem. So, he was looking for neem leaves. Bathing in warm water with neem leaves cures children's skin diseases. Therefore, he was searching for a neem tree. It is difficult to get neem leaves in Bengaluru. He remembered that, in the park near their previous house, there was a big neem tree. Last Saturday he went to that park to fetch neem leaves. But he was amazed, what he saw there. The five-acre park no longer remained a park. It had become a place of worship. Goddes Mangamma has appeared there.

There is a large round granite stone with a big hole in the middle of it near an anthill inside the park. A platform is erected near the anthill with a shamiana above it. A ten to twelve year old girl is sitting on that platform. She wears a champak colour saree with red boarder and having a large vermilion circular mark on her forehead. There is a long line of people in front of her, so long that, it is eye-popping. One by one they are coming and touching her feet. She is also blessing them. In front of her is a brass plate of about three feet diameter. The devotees are offering money as per their wish. Some are even donating gold and silver. Coconuts, bananas are offered to the Goddess and milk poured in that stone pit. Manoj was surprised to see all this but when he saw a twenty feet high photo near the anthill, his eyes widened. Even if he tried, he could not close his eye lids. The photo is of Mother Mangamma. In that photo, a beautiful woman is wearing a champak colour saree with wide red boarder and a big vermilion Circular mark on her forehead. Her left hand is extended towards four women who are prostrating before her and the right hand towards that black granite rock from whose hole a huge black cat is drinking milk. Two bangles are on her both wrists and the photo is not of any other person but of his mother i.e. Archana's.

Archana opened the e-mail attachment. She was shocked to see the photo. This is her photograph. But how is this possible?

She recalled. About eight months ago, she had been to her daughter's house at Hyderabad. After returning from there, she also stayed a few days in her son's house at Bengaluru. During that time, one day she had gone to the nearby park for a walk alone. She remembers well that she was wearing that champak coloured saree with red border. While walking in the park, she saw four women were tying thread around an anthill. They were worshipping near that anthill by keeping coconuts and bananas and pouring milk in the middle of the nearby round granite rock. She was sitting on a cement bench and watching it. She was thinking, what short of worship it could be? She was very much worried seeing so much milk being wasted and coconuts, bananas piled up there in the name of goddess. She could not tolerate it. She collected all those coconuts and bananas and gave them to the beggars sitting outside the park. Then she started walking on the walking track. She saw that those women were standing at a distance and talking something among themselves and meanwhile a cat was drinking that milk continuously. She thought that she should explain to the women not to waste so much food. She went to them and tried to explain that matter by gesture because they were unable to understand Odia. She also pointed her hand to show them the cat drinking the milk. Suddenly, for some unknown reasons, all four of them knelt down and bowed their heads before her. Without understanding anything and thinking that any untoward incident may happen, she slipped out through the nearby gate and hurriedly returned home. At that time, perhaps someone had taken a photo and after a few editing made a photo like this on the computer.

Archana rang Manoj. She said, "The photo looks like mine. But how can this be mine? This must be someone with a similar face. You know that there are at least six persons resembling one's face on this earth."

The voice of Manoj from the other end, "But Mama! So many coincidences at the same time! This is completely impossible. The photograph has your face, wearing your saree, the same large vermilion circular mark of yours and also those bulky Redstone fitted bangles of yours. All these indicates that this is your photo. I am very much worried. They may implicate you in this matter in future. Apart from that, what will be the future of that little, innocent girl? This must be the work of a criminal group. By propagating lies to the common innocent people, by giving false assurances, by showing them false dream, they are making huge income every day. This is one kind of fraud." Gradually Manoj was getting excited.

Archana pacified him and said, "Do not worry. I will tell this matter to your father and see what can be done. You try to inquire something about this matter during this time. Here, I am also talking with your father."

Archana put the phone down. She washed her face and drank a glass of water and thought about our society.

Our people are so religious and god fearing that if someone puts a stone under a tree, coats vermilion on it, offers flowers, sandalwood paste and burns some incense sticks, then the people passing by that road will bow down there and give a few pennies. Our people have a lot of faith. The clinic of Dr Sahu in our city is always very crowded. One has to go early in the morning to collect a token. The serial number for meeting the doctor is given as per the token number. Because the people have deep faith on him. Once you go to him, your disease must be cured, His medicines are very effective. It really happens. The same medicine prescribed by other doctors does not work so effectively. This is only the result of faith. And the difference between faith and superstition is very thin. Here too that belief or superstition is at work. If a person believes that by going to Ma Mangamma, his wish will be fulfilled or the disease will be cured, then his self-confidence will increase and as a result ultimately his work will be successful or the disease will be cured.

After Debendra Came, Archana raised the matter. He got upset by hearing that. He said, "Why were you involved in all this? You had gone for a few days. What was the necessity to enter into all these complicacies. Those are outside our place." Then he said in a calm voice, "Ok. I am trying to gather some information on this matter. I have become friends with many people while staying with our son there. I have also their phone numbers. I am trying to find out about this by calling them."

After one week ....

Manoj telephoned and said, "There is a village existing around thirty five kilometres from Mandya town in Karnataka. It's name is Bekalel. The main goddess of that village is Cat. They called her Devi Mangamma.

For thousands of years they have been worshipping this Mangamma. There are three temples in their village where statues of cats are installed. There is a folktale that where goddess Mangamma appeared in the form of a Cat and disappeared after saving them, suddenly there surfaced an anthill. Ma Mangamma's festival is also held in about three to four years intervals. The village priest calculated and determines the auspicious days for the festival. The festival lasted for about four days. The last fair was in 2014. No one mistreats cats in that village. Whoever does it gets punishment. If a man accidentally sees the dead body of a cat, he burns it and goes anywhere after that only."

Archana knew that worshipping cats as goddess is not a new thing. She read that cats were worshiped as goddesses in Egypt about five thousand years ago. At that time, their name was Baset or Sekhmet.

Manoj spoke again, "The house of the person in charge of the park is in that Bekalel Village. On that day some guests from his village came to him. There were four women among them. When they saw a beautiful, lustrous woman (as per their view) distributing coconuts, bananas, which were already offered by them, to the beggars, they felt that she is not an ordinary woman. And when you showed them, by the gesture of your hand, the cat drinking milk, they believed that Goddess Mangamma had appeared in the anthill. So they fell on their knees and bowed down to you. As you had escaped in that moment, they thought that goddess Mangamma had disappeared. The cat also ran away. After that they started worshipping. Some day's passed like this. Gradually the number of people increased. One day it was announced that goddess Mangamma had appeared in the body of a teenage girl. A pandal was built overnight. And from the next day the young girl surfaced there in a half awakened and half-conscious state. It was propagated that, those who touch Mangamma's feet and beg for her blessings will surely have their wishes fulfilled. People are queuing there in faith. Money, gold, silver are being poured in to the puja plate."

Every day the worship is starting from seven in the morning. There is a rest of two hours in the afternoon. Then the Puja continues until eight o' clock at night. The huge puja ashet is getting full.

It seems to me, Mama! , that this is the work of a group of mischievous people. Luring with money, a girl from a poor family has been brought and placed there. A state of hypnosis has been created by giving her a low dose of intoxicating substances or drugs. She does not say anything to anyone. She is blessing by raising her hands as per the direction of the fat priest sitting next to her. Among the people who are coming, some people's prayers are automatically fulfilled. For example, some of the women who desire a son must have a son. The persons whose wishes are fulfilled, further propagates her glory. Many innocent people are falling into this trap. It is absolutely necessary to stop it.

In fact, it is unequivocally essential to prevent it. Archana hung up the phone.

She consulted with Debendra. She took out the prints of the mail and photo through him. Next day, she met the Bhubaneswar police Commissioner and explained everything in detail. The Police commissioner also called the Bengaluru Police Commissioner and informed everything. The Police Commissioner of Bengaluru requested Archana to come to Bengaluru as a guest of Karnataka Government. The day was also fixed.

On the appointed day Archana landed at the

Bengaluru airport. The Police vehicle came to pick her up. Archana narrated her experiences at a big press conference arranged by the police. Before that, the police arrested all the members of that notorious gang. And crores of rupees along with gold, silver were recovered from them. The most important thing was, the innocent girl was rescued.

Archana was thinking, "Many such incidents are seen in our society. Many monks, nuns, cheaters, crooks are planning to became millionaires and billionaires overnight. Common innocent people are also getting caught in their scams and losing their hard earned money."

The trust of anybody should not be breached. But the belief that turns into superstition and thousands of people are robbed by it, it is the duty of every conscious citizen to break that belief and turn it into disbelief.

***

"Blind belief can be comforting, but it can easily cripple reason and productivity, and stop intellectual progress." - James Randi

The Star in A Moonlit Night

The sun has already set beyond the distance horizon since long. The darkness has started its reign. The electric lights on all the electric poles in the city have been switched on. "Kala Mandap", the best auditorium in the city, is decorated like a new bride. The place is very crowded in this evening. There is no place even to throw a mustard. The lower hall and the upper balcony are full of people. Still some people are standing in the back. The Kalamandap is shaking with resounding applause after every announcement. Today, people who have achieved success in various fields in the state are being felicitated. The Chief Minister of the state and other dignitaries have come. Awards have already been given to the best artists, poets, writers, doctors etc. The last one is the highest civic honour. Although the Governor of the state is the first citizen, but the best citizen is he who has become a favourite of the countless people of the state by his exemplary dedicated service. Accordingly, various institutions have recommended the names of around ten people. The person who gets the most votes from the public, will get the highest civic honour today. Everyone's mind is anxious, who is the great personality who has won the hearts of the people of the state. After a pause, the announcer came up to the stage and said, "the last award of the day is the best civic honour. He also announced the names of the ten recommended people. As each name was announced, their faces were displayed on the big screen placed on the stage. The anxiety of the public continued to grow. Finally, the announcer announced, " the highest civilian honoree has won by a landslide margin. She is non other than honourable Radharani Devi. The pavilion shook with applause. Again the announcer's voice-requesting her to come up to the stage, accept the honour and speak a few words to guide us.

The theatre hall erupted in applause. The people rose from their seats and clapped to welcome Radharani Devi as she got up from her seat and walked on to the stage.

Radharani Devi is standing on the stage. Age should be above sixty. Colour is neither white nor black. As if the love, affection and compassion are pouring from her face. She is dressed in a simple cotton saree. In it, she looks glorious. A person will want to respect her at the first sight.

The Chief Minister has already honoured her. Now she will say something. There is total silence in the hall. Even if a leaf falls, it's sound will be heard. She began her speech after greeting everyone.

I have been asked to say on two things today. Firstly my biography and secondly from whom I got inspiration to excel myself in this social service. I will tell. It might be a little longer. Please excuse me for that. Because I am going to present to you another character. She took some time, cleared her throat and began.

A girl was wandering in the alleys of Bhubaneswar in the sizzling summer in the month of May. Some books and a bag were in her hands. That was a Sunday. Generally, fish or motton were cooked at the homes and the people must have enjoyed their food and relaxed. But the girl went from house to house ringing the calling bell and requesting feverishly to buy a book. Perhaps her luck was not favourable. It was already one PM. But not a single book could be sold. Her throat seemed to dry up due to extreme hunger, thirst and heat. No... she could not proceed any more. Even there was no water tap nearby to drink some water. She thought that she would go to the nearby house and ask for some water. She entered the house by opening the gate and rang the calling bell.

An old woman opened the door. By that time the girl was totally exhausted. She said, "aunty, please give me some water. My throat is drying up due to this extreme hot summer."

The woman looked at her and thought that "these people are coming in the noon time of the day and are cheating and even killing people in the name of selling." She is a lonely woman. Suppressing the fear in her mind, she looked to the girl more intently. How old will the girl be? Twenty or twenty two. Very weak body. She was sweating profusely and looked very tired. As if she was not in a position to stand. She felt pity for her. What will happen will be seen later. She called her inside and asked her to sit on a chair and switched on the fan. She brought water in a bottle and gave it to her. The girl took the bottle and started drinking. After drinking half of the bottle, she felt a little better. She looked at the old lady and said, "thank you aunty. I was totally fatigued due to this extreme heat."

"How can one come out in this hot summer? The Government has made a rule that no one will work after eleven O'clock. And what are you doing? Selling the books? How did your parents leave you in this circumstances? Have you eaten anything or roaming in an empty stomach?"

The girl was looking to the old lady with astonishment. Usually people are keeping distance from her. They buy something or not, could not they say it nicely? But this woman is a unique person. The girl's eyes became moist at such sweet and lovely words of her. The emotions inside her mind could no longer be checked. Tears flowed from her eyes as if the dam had burst and the water flowed rapidly and aimlessly.

Hey! Hey! what happened? Why are you crying? The old lady was worried.

The girl wiped her eyes and said, "aunty ! I have never seen my mother, who gave me birth and the soil where I took birth, in my life. I was born in an unknown village in Dhenkanal District. When I was two years old my mother died of an unknown disease. My father became alone. Everybody forced him to marry for a second time on the plea that the new wife will take care of the girl. But father did not agree at all. Grandma and grandpa were very upset. They told clearly that they will not give any property unless he marries again. Their desire was, to have a son by marrying my father again. But father did not see any difference between son and daughter. He did not study much but his mind was very broad. He loved me very much, even though I was a girl. If he remarries, I may be neglected, abused. That's why he did not agree to the marriage and was looking for an opportunity to get rid of this problem. Soon he got that chance. A friend of my father was doing a small job in Bhubaneswar. After discussing with him, he came to Bhubaneswar with me. At first we stayed at his house for a few days. Their house was in a slum area. It was on a Government land and having tin sheets on the mud walls. However, after working a few days as a Labourer, he got a job as a peon in a private school. Father had built another mud house near his friend's house. We are living in that house till date. At first, I was taken care by Ketaki aunty. My father's friend's wife is a very nice person. She was taking care of me after dad went to office. Gradually

I grew up. I studied in the nearby Government School. In spite of all the hardship, God has given me a great blessing. That is my memory power. What I was reading was remembered at once. I stood first in all the classes and passed with good marks in tenth as well. Then college. My father was fulfilling all my needs. He used to praise me in front of his friends, saying, "See, my daughter will be famous one day." I also read sincerely.

Father's health had deteriorated during my final year of B. A. His right side became immobile due to paralysis. We had to stay in the hospital for two months. The doctor said that it happened due to excessive diabetes. After taking the medicine, the diabetes subsided but his hands and feet became motionless: He is doing his daily routine works with much difficulties. Our situation worsened due to the ill health of my father. Whatever little savings we had, were gone for staying in the hospital and buying the medicines. At first the slum dwellers were helping us to some extent. That too was stopped. How much they can afford with their pitiable financial condition.

We were totally penniless. Hungry stomach, empty pocket and broken heart teach the greatest lessons in life. During this period I had completed my B.A. and applied for M. A. I had a hope that I could get a lecturer job if somehow I would pass M.A. in English. But for that money was required. After a lot of searching, now I am doing a part time job in a big shop and selling these books on Saturdays and Sundays. I am getting a commission of fifty rupees for each book I sell. You know, fifty rupees is a big amount for us. We can manage two days with it. I thought that once a book is sold, I will buy rice, potato and some other things. But nothing could be sold today. I gave my father a little stale rice water to drink. Tears flowed from the eyes of the girl. The old lady's eyes also got wet. Perhaps, she was thinking about the people living in extreme hardship.

She went inside and brought a glass of butter milk for her to drink and also bought a book from her. She put some rice, flattened rice, potatoes, sugar and biscuits in a polythene bag and gave it to her. She said, come hear whenever you come to this side. I will purchase your book. The girl was verymuch grateful on that day. She was thinking, "there are still such helpful and kind hearted people existing in this world."

Do you know who was that pious lady? She was Kanak Manjari Pattnaik and that girl is standing in front of you, that means me.

Everyone was staring in total silence.

Wiping her face Radharani Devi said again. On that first meeting with Kanak Devi on that day, I was verymuch impressed by her sweet demeanour and sacrificing nature. She had told me to buy books whenever I will go there.

Next Sunday I went there with my bag full of books. I visited her. She was very happy. She asked me to sitdown and purchased a book. She paid the price of the book and gave me extra three thousand rupees along with it. As I looked at her with surprise, she said, "You are now continuing your M.A. course. It will take two years to complete it. Money must be needed for it. So keep this money. You may repay it after getting a job. She brought a notebook and kept a note of it. She also said, "whenever you require money, please come and take it. All will be noted. You will repay it later." She knew my condition. Still she was eager to help me. I learned from her, how much joy one gets by giving. I looked at her face. There was absolutely no ill intention. There was no desire to get anything but only helping attitude.

Always money is needed. Two more times I brought money from her. She also gave me unhesitatingly. Always she used to say "read mindfully." I was thanking God in my heart. Truly, as God has brought us to this earth, He has also arranged how our life will be sustained. Otherwise, I would not have met Kanak Devi in the critical juncture of my life.

I completed my M.A. I stood first class first. I had worked very hard for it. Because, I knew that my future depends on my examination result.

I got a Lecturer job verysoon. Now the time has come to repay the money borrowed from Kanak Devi gradually. After receiving the first month's salary, I went to her house. She was very happy to hear about my job. When I returned the money, she refused to accept it. She said, "I knew you would come to return the money. But I did not give it to take it back. I was noting it on a notebook so that your self respect would not be hurt. That was my capital that I invested in you. If you can use this money to help some needy, helpless people then that will be your debt relief. By way of talking, I got to know something about her life on that day. In truth, only those who grow up struggling in life can understand the life and feel the pain of others.

After returning that day, I made up my mind. I would sacrifice everything to help the needy and poor people. I kept the affection-coated money that I brought back from her in a separate place. I decided in my heart that I will spend a certain part of my monthly salary for the poor. But I kept looking for the needy people so as not to give charity in vain. In the hospital, I arranged medicines for those patients who were unable to purchase. I helped the students in colleges who could not pay their tuition fees due to their proverty. Slowly the joy of giving like this absorbed my body and mind. The experience of so much joy and self satisfaction in giving brought heavenly joy to my mind. The mind became anxious to do something for the neglected, oppressed, exploited people in the society.

I had gone to Kanak Devi's house after about six months. By that time she was bed ridden. Her two sons and daughters-in-Law who were staying away, had come. Treatment was going on. She was happy to see me. She said, "I wanted to see you. Anyway you have come."

I said, "Mother! I have used the capital, you have given me in right way. That capital continues to grow. I have decided to spend my whole life in the service of the society. You are my guide and inspiration. The main aim of my life will be the betterment of the society. I have taken two decisions for the welfare of the society. First I will remove my title by means of an affidavit. A person's title often reveals his clan, tradition and from that comes a sense of respect or contempt for him. I want to build a caste free society. The scriptures we follow like Gita, Mahabharat, Ramayan did not have such titles. Be it Sri Ramachandra or Ravan in Ramayan or Yudhisthir, Sri Krishna, Duryodhan in Mahabharat, they had no titles. So why should we? Let everyone be equal in this society. I urge the young men and women of this generation to abandon their titles. As a result, the next generation can become a completely casteless society.

Secondly, I will not marry. Marriage is a happy bond. It has a prime responsibility towards the family. For me this whole society is my family. I do not want to be confined to a small family.

Hearing my words, Kanak Devi's face lit up with happiness. She blessed me with a hand gesture. I came back touching her feet.

After some days Kanak Devi left for her eternal abode. She was a star in a moonlit night. The stars are not visible on a moonlit night. But they are stars those shine brilliantly for ever. They are far greater than the moon. Like that, a towering personality like Kanak Devi had helped so many needy and helpless people like me, remaining totally unknown, behind the screen of the society. There are so many Kanak Manjari Davis in our society. This world is moving on for them only. It was under her inspiration that this great institution stands today, from which thousands of children have been educated and established in every nook and corner of the earth. They have also brought international fame in sports. My one and only request to them is that they should help others. I expect this number to rise to lakhs and lakhs. And in this society, there will be no one who is neglected, oppressed or victimised. Thank you all.

At first there was silence for a while. Then the auditorium resounded with loud applause.

***

"It is easier to take than to give. It is nobler to give than to take. The thrill of taking lasts a day. The thrill of giving lasts a life time." - Joan Marques

The Restive Afternoon

Explosion! Explosion! A massive explosion. But this explosion is not from any bomb nor from any ammunition nor from any explosive device. This is the explosion of sentences, explosion of sound and explosion of words. In this explosion no buildings, bridges or dams are destroyed but by this all the tissues inside the heart are severely damaged. Many bridges of relationship fall apart. Destroyed dams, buildings can be reconstructed but the damaged nerves and ruined relationships can no longer be repaired.

This is what happened in Anil's house. Son Amar and daughter-in-law Ava complained that Ava's gold jewelleries had disappeared from this house. It was not a complain but an accusation. Ava insisted that the ornaments had been stolen from this house only.

This is how it took place. Amar and Abha are married for two and half years. After one month of their marriage, they had gone to Bengaluru, the work place of Amar. Ava took all her jewelleries with her. Mother-in-law Asima had advised, "why should you carry around so much ornaments, keep them here in the locker." Ava listened it but ignored. Asima also did not insist her. Their possessions, let them do what they please. Meanwhile, they are blessed with a son. Asima was in Bengaluru for a few days when their son was born.

Now after a long gap they have returned to

Bhubaneswar. They will stay here for a few days and attend a marriage ceremony. They were coming by train from Bengaluru. On the way the little son fell ill. So as soon as they arrived, they were busy in visiting the doctor. The paternal house of the daughter-in-law is at Puri. A reputed paediatrician was well known to her father. That's why they took their son to Puri immediately. After staying for four to five days and after the little son getting better, they have returned.

Tomorrow, there will be a marriage function. She wanted the jewellery packet to see which ornament to wear. But when she opened the trolley bag for the jewellery packet, it was not there. Only then this violent explosion took place. Ava's view was that all the gold ornaments has been stolen from this house. Anil tried his level best to explain her "you have journeyed all the way by the train, again you have gone to Puri and stayed there for so many days and all along the bag was with you. Therefore, it is difficult to know where the gold ornaments are lost or stolen. How can you tell that it has been stolen from this house? who else is here? There are two of us and the widow aunty. Can any one of us steal the ornaments? We have gifted more than half of the ornaments at the time of marriage. Then remains the aunty. What she will do with jewellery or money. Apart from it, why are you worried so much if the jewelleries are stolen? Some gold were lost but not our fortune. We will purchase some more ornaments."

Asima also explained everything. But Ava was not in a position to hear anything. She strongly believes that the gold jewelleries have been stolen from this house. If you search, you will find them inside this house. She again said "these are my wedding ornaments. The jewellery given by my parents and gifted by others are about 150 grams. Apart from the value, many people's sentiments are involved. No matter how much ornaments you buy, those will never come back. Again, gold to be stolen or lost is ominous. It is a sign of one's impending misfortune."

Anil was compelled to make a phone call to Ava's father. Requested both of them to come here and make Ava understand the matter. If some gold is lost then it does not mean the end of the world or affect their status. May be their daughter will accept her parent's counselling.

But the parents of Ava are totally disinterested. His words had no effect on them. Her father flatly refused and said, "we should not go at all." It will be like "between Scylla and Charybdis" or "between the devil and deep blue sea." What can we say to anyone? Besides when she is not listening to you, how she will listen to us? Therefore, please excuse us."

But Anil could not understand the mentality and behaviour of the new age children. The children born between 1981 to 1996 are called millennials and those born between 1996 to 2012 are called Generation Z. By the time they were born, the computer age had already begun. There had been an unforeseen revolution in the field of communication. They consider themselves as children of a different era.

They do not have the same respect and courtesy we had for our parents and elders during our time. Even though we were engaged in jobs and had become a father, we could not raise our heads and speak loudly in front of our father. If we had to say something to our father, we used to convey it through our mother. Now the children have no respect for the elders. They treat their fathers like common friends. They think that they know everything. Parents are fools. Whether the father is a doctor, engineer, professor etc these positions or qualifications have no value before today's children. In no way the children's thoughts, activities, and preferences match those of their parents. This may be due to lack of healthy communications. Today's children do not listen stories from their grandparents anymore. There is no time to spend with parents. All are busy with computer, laptop, mobile etc. Apart from study, they have to devote time for many other activities like dancing, singing, swimming etc. As both the parents are service holders, they are unable to spare time for their children. The child will grow up either with a nanny or in a day care home. There is no mutual exchange of ideas with each other. How can affection and closeness develop?

"Hello! why are you sitting so quietly? Speak to the children, do something." Anil came to senses by Asima's words. For a long time, he was wondering, what is happening. He called Amar and Ava again and tried to make them realise the situation. It is futile to cry over spilt milk. So, Stop worrying over that matter. He told to Amar, "You go. Buy some ornaments for the daughter-in-law. I am giving the required money."

But Ava was unyielding and said, "I must expose the one who took my gold ornaments." It was clear that Amar was supporting Ava though he did not say anything directly. He said, "father! I am going to police station to lodge an F.I.R. In a case of theft from the house, it is necessary to lodge complain with the police."

Anil remarked, "After lodging FIR, the police will come and interrogate the members of the house. Then the house will be searched. I know very well that the gold ornaments are not stolen from here. Therefore, gold will not be found but we will be disgraced in the neighbourhood only."

Ava insisted, "Dad! Why are you saying that the gold will not be found. Gold may be inside this house."

Anil was shocked. What do you mean? we have three rooms in the house. One room is yours, another is ours and the third one is your auntie's (Anil's sister) There is no gold in your room. Then do you think that it will be in our room or auntie Arundhati's room.

Immediately Ava responded, "Why in your room. I think, if we will search auntie's room, probably we will find it."

What! Anil was stunned for a moment. What Ava is talking about? She is directly hinting at Arundhati and Amar did not protest even after hearing. That means he Is also...

Today's children are speaking straight. They will say whatever they think. But for that they have to consider the time, place and the person about whom they are speaking. It is also important to pay attention to the mentality and emotion of others.

He looked towards the door. Has Arundhati heard this? Then he told Ava, "Have you thought of what you are speaking? I will never let this happen. I do not want to add more pain to a grief-stricken person. Do whatever you think. Lodge FIR with police. Let the police come. All rooms should be searched. Again, I will suggest that your Puri house should also be inspected thoroughly. Then if you get the gold, it is yours. If not, nothing will happen. Now please go from here. Do whatever you want to do." Anil was raging with anger. But the fiery flame of anger was extinguished by a calm and sweet voice. Anil saw Arundhati standing in front of him. She said, "brother! Let Amar and Ava do what they want to do. I have no objection. They are youngsters. If there is any doubt in their mind, then it should be removed."

"But they are going to make a big mistake," - Anil's painful voice.

Arundhati continued in the same nonchalant voice, "It is normal for the children to make mistakes. They will learn from those mistakes. And regarding us, if a child defecates sitting on his father's lap, then does the father cut off his thigh and throw it away? Rather he cleans his son carefully and also his thigh. Like that, give them a chance to clean the soot in their mind."

Then, Arundhati had heard everything! How she would not hear? He was talking in such a loud voice.

All the incidents of the past were floating in his mind's eye. Arundhati is younger by two and half years to him. While she was reading in the college, a good marriage alliance was proposed. Good family and the boy was a lecturer. They liked Arundhati and wanted an early marriage. Parents also consented to it. Their daughter will stay happy. But who can resist the cruel wheel of time? Her husband died in an accident only after a year of her marriage. Our father wanted to bring her back home after the funeral rites were over. His intention to bring her home was to start her study again and ultimately get her re-married. But Arundati refused. She decided to stay there only. Her husband's family was also her family. Father came back. He was very much in pain. How unfortunate she was! Indeed, only the calamities are written in the fortune of some people. Why does it happen so? Is it the result of previous birth's actions? Is there any previous birth? What is the need to suffer the fruits of previous birth's activities in this birth? Whereas one does not remember his previous birth at all. The people will probably be reformed if the birth in which one had sinned had reaped the fruits. Leave it, these are all big things. And ordinary person does not have the capacity to think all this. Let her stay there if she wants so.

But after a year, it was reported that Arundhati was not doing well there. Arundhati never complained anything. Hearing from outsiders, father became worried. Her in-laws were torturing her. They were blaming her for their son's death. After hearing all this, which father can stay patiently? Suddenly, one day he went to their house. Anil also had accompanied him. Arundhati was beyond recognition. Her appearance had totally changed within a year only. Healthy, strong and fair like turmeric Arundhati looked weak, withered and dishevelled. There was a vast difference between Arundhati of one year back and Arundhati of today. A dirty cloth was on her body. Father was very angry. There were altercations and uproar there. They left the house with Arundhati at that moment. No one from her in-law's house stopped her. Perhaps, they were thinking, it was better if she left. Their burden would be lightened. The issue of how the definition of relationship changes over time, disturbs the mind.

Since then, Arundhati has been staying in this house. The parents tried to get her married again. Now-a-days widow marriage has been a common thing. But Arundhati did not agree at all.

A few days before his marriage, his father called him. Mother was also present there. Father said, "Look Anil! After a few days you will be married. A daughter-in-law will come to our home. It is a common thing that after the son's marriage there is some changes in the ambience of the house. Because, an entirely new girl comes from a different background. If she is good-natured then the house will become a heaven. And if she is ill-tempered then there will be always disturbances in the house. We have also

Arundhati at our home. She is very unfortunate. Let no one neglect her. I have transferred some land in her name. I also kept some money in the bank for her. However, it is the support and co-operation of one's family rather than money that brings peace of mind. As long as we live, I will not allow to make her suffer. But after us, you have to take her responsibilities. She should not be neglected in the least. Consider this as our last wish."

On that day, he burst into tears with emotion. Placing his hand on his father's hand he vowed to keep Arundhati happy always. After his marriage, he expressed his inner feelings to wife Asima. Asima also happily accepted Arundhati whole heartedly. In the process of time, father and mother passed away. Asima never ignored Arundhati. The relationship between the two was not limited to sisters-in-law but it was a deep friendship. They were openly talking to each other. They were sharing one another's happiness and sorrowness. While constructing this house, Anil kept Arundhati in mind and built a three-bedroom house. Arundhati stays with him till to day. There never is any difficulty or difference of opinion. But today what is happening? Why is this storm of discontent rising in the afternoon of life? In this ripe age the man wants nothing else but peace, healthy environment, love for each other. Cannot this fire of unrest be extinguished? Will not the cold stream of peace flow?

But Arundhati was unfazed. She was calling everyone to search her room. Anil got up even though he did not want it. He said to Amar and Ava. "Go! Search her room. Find out the gold ornaments." Without saying a word, both of them entered Arundhati's room and searched everything minutely. Nothing was found. Finally, Ava's eyes fell on a large wooden box with a large lock hanging on it. Ava was sure that her gold ornaments must be inside that box. As soon as she looked at Arundhati's face, Arundhati handed her the key of the box.

Ava took the key and opened the box. There were only a few pieces of sarees in that big box. But Ava's suspicious mind could not comprehend, why such a big lock for a few pieces of sarees? There must be something inside. She brought out the sarees one by one. There was a tin box at the bottom of that big box. That was also locked. Ava was very happy. Her eyes shone brightly. Her ornaments must be in that box. She asked Arundhati for the keys. Anil was also confused for a moment. He has never seen such a box. And what is the meaning of being so carefully hidden and locked. He prayed God from the bottom of his heart that Ava's suspicions would not turn out to be true. The next moment he took control of himself. What is he thinking? After being with her for so many years, has he not understood her character? He looked forward and saw that Arundhati is handling over a key to Ava.

Ava grabbed the key and quickly opened the lock. But what is this? There was no gold inside the box. Ava strewed all the things kept inside the box. Anil saw that there were some wedding photos of Arundhati and a single photo of her husband. Tears came to Anil's eyes. He could not bear it anymore. He said to Ava, "Have you seen everything? Now stop all this rubbish."

Amar and Ava were also little bit disheartened. They probably felt guilty for not getting anything. Amar was going to collect and keep all the photos. But Arundhati said, "I will keep all my things in order, if your work is over, you can go."

Everyone went away quickly. There was a tense atmosphere in the house. No cooking was done in the night, no one ate anything. Ava only brought warm milk for her son. He is a child of one and half years. What does he know. It is still a few years before the world's complicity enters his mind. Everyone went to their rooms to sleep. Anil also lay on his bed. But where is the sleep? His mind was getting heavy. He was thinking that, after this incident, can everyone in the house will be normal with each other? As the time went by, early in the morning, his eyes closed a little.

He was awakened by the noise in the morning. In drowsiness, he came out of his room. Amar's friend Prakash is standing in the nearby dining hall and speaking something. Everyone is listening attentively with keen interest.

Hey Prakash! You came so early in the morning.

Hearing Anil's voice, Prakash greeted him and said, "Uncle! Please see an Odia news in T.V. you can know everything."

By that time Amar had already started the T.V. After changing two or four channels, they saw some news were scrolling below. It was written there that, "It has been informed by the police that on the 8th of this month some gold ornaments wrapped in a piece of red cloth were recovered from a woman who had stolen it from Jaswantpur-Bhubaneswar express train, whoever owns these ornaments can take it from Brahmapur railway police station by providing proper proof."

Prakash is a good friend of Amar. Amar must have told him about the theft of gold ornaments. So, after knowing the incident, he came running.

Ava had a strong belief that those are her ornaments. Because she and Amar had wrapped the gold ornaments in a salu kana (red cloth). But they did not understand one thing that the packet was in the bottom of the trolley bag. Then how it was stolen? Anyway, they have to go to Brahmapur and check it. But what proof we will give - Amar asked Anil.

Anil said, "the bill of the diamond ring that was given to Ava at the time of her engagement is still with me. The jewellery shopkeeper told that the bill will be required at the time of exchange of the diamond ring. There may be some bills of gold ornaments purchased at the time of marriage. I have to search them. But the greatest proof is your wedding albums and CDs. It contains the photos of the ornaments worn by Ava."

Anyway, taking photo albums, CDs and some jewellery bills, Amar and Ava took a taxi and left for Brahmapur. After about three hours they reached Brahmapur railway police station. They showed the bills and photos to the inspector there. The photos showed the clear pictures of large necklaces. The inspector went inside brought a packet from the store room. As soon as Ava saw the red cloth wrapped packet, she screamed "this is the packet." The inspector also verified the photos and bills and was sure that the ornaments belonged to them. A list of ornaments was made. Amar and Ava signed some written documents. Then only the ornaments were handed over to them.

Amar thanked the inspector and asked, "How did you suspect and catch that woman?"

The inspector replied, "There had been an increase in theft from trains at this Brahmapur railway station during the last few days. Therefore, we were a bit cautious. We often saw this man and women inside the station. There was also a little doubt on them. That day as soon as the train left the station, both of them got off the train with the red packet and went out hurriedly. We brought them to the police station on suspicion. When we verified, we detected the gold ornaments inside the packet. After a couple of slaps, they admitted that they had stolen it." Without delay, they returned in the same taxi.

Ava was thinking on the way back, "How was this possible? How did someone notice the packet at the bottom of the bag?" She said to Amar, "see! It could be like this. When our son got sick with fever and dysentery, we were very much worried. We had decided to give medicine without delay. But the medicines were kept at the bottom of the trolley bag. I opened the trolley bag inside the train and removed the upper clothes one by one and then took out the medicine box from the bottom of the bag. Do you remember? There was a woman sitting next to us. As the son was crying loudly and consistently, she took him from you and swung him in her arms. She also helped me while packing the bag. All attention was on our son. We did not focus on other things. Taking advantages of our inattentiveness, the woman must have given that packet to her male friend. Then they got down comfortably when the train started leaving the station. But unfortunately, they were caught by the police. As far as I remember, I did not see that woman after Brahmapur station. Leave it! We got our stuff that is a big thing."

After the initial excitement of finding the ornaments subsided, it dawned on Ava and Amar what a grievous mistake they had made. The insistence of Ava that the gold ornaments were stolen from the house and searching of Arundhati's room proved to be a big blunder. How will they go home now and show their faces before others. The closer the taxi got to Bhubaneswar, the more their state of mind became afflicted. Finally, the taxi stopped in front of their house.

Amar had informed earlier the news of recovery of ornaments. Now both of them entered the house slowly with the packet.

Anil was sitting on his usual chair in the drawing room with a newspaper in his hand. Amar went and gently placed the packet at Anil's feet and stood silently. He did not have courage to say anything. Ava's face was completely off white

Anil looked at both of them. But that look was completely unconcerned, He said, "the gold ornaments recovered. Now go." He told only this much. Amar could feel how badly his father was hurt. Asima reached at that time.

Both Amar and Ava fell at their feet. They confessed, "we have done a mistake. A very big mistake! We were out of our wits as the gold ornaments were stolen. This type of mistake will never happen again. Please forgive us this time."

While Asima was picking them up, Anil said, "we will forgive you. But are you really unable to know anything? Before you say something, pointing your fingers to someone, think twice. Her life has already been destroyed. All smiles and happiness are lost. What will she do with gold ornaments in this afternoon of her life? A little peace is required for her. You know, she has not eaten anything since you left. She sat before God for a long time. Her only wish was that your ornaments be found and she should be free from any stigma. Apologise to her if you can. How much pain you have given her."

Both of them went to Arundhati's room. They saw their son was playing in Arundhati's lap. The eyes of Arundhati were swollen. Perhaps she cried a lot. Both held her feet and begged her forgiveness. Tears were flowing from their eyes. Arundhati also wept. All the blocked discontentment's, resentments were coming out in shape of tears. Seeing the tears of three, the little son must have thought something and laughed. He was trying to touch Arundhati's eyes with his tiny hands as if saying, "do not cry. Everything will be alright. The storm has petered out. The restive afternoon has now calmed down."

**

"The afternoon of a human life must have a significance of its own, and can not be merely a pitiful appendage of Life's morning."

- C. G. Jung

The Only Mistake

No one can live his entire life flawlessly. Somewhere he stumbles. As if, making mistakes is his natural instinct. He will do something wrong knowingly or unknowingly. A prudent person corrects the mistakes and regrets later. Some even make atonements. It is normal for humans to make mistakes. But a mistake committed deliberately with planning is not a mistake but a crime. There is no atonement for that mistake. He should be punished.

But he does not want to be punished. There is also the fear of public shame. Therefore, he has to hide the mistake. But to hide his mistake, he has to make another mistake. Further to hide it again an additional mistake. A long list of mistakes will follow. Will he succeed? "A thief's house is not always dark". What will happen in the end? All these thoughts were running in Adinath's mind.

He was reminiscing about the incidents happened in the past. Adinath is an employee of Rourkela Steel Plant. It is a good job, good salary. After a long search he married Arati only three years back. She has a twin sister, Aditi. The appearance of the two sisters are so alike that the outsiders cannot easily identify who is Arati and who is Aditi. Adinath himself has also confused many times. After a year of their marriage, the marriage of Aditi was Solmnised with lecturer Abhijeet. They have a daughter of one year old. Adinath also has a two-year-old daughter. Llike this their family life was running. It was also running smoothly.

About fifteen days ago they came to Rourkela to visit Adinath's house. After touring some places in Rourkela, they plan to visit Badaghagara falls. Badaghagara is around one hundred twenty kilo meters away from Rourkela. They hired an Inova car on rent and went to Badaghagara on one Sunday. The scenic natural beauty of Badaghagara had mesmerized them. But after returning, Aditi fell sick. She had high fever and her entire body was aching. Adinath's steel plant has its own hospital named Ispat General Hospital (IGH). So he immediately took Aditi and got her admitted there. There he made the mistake. What a man does not ever think, what he never dreamt of doing, at times he does it. Is it the effect of planetary constellation? At that moment, due to the transit of any planet in his zodiac sign and its influence, he took this kind of decision.

A strange idea came to the mind of Adinath when Aditi was admitted in the hospital. He thought that if he will admit Aditi in the hospital as his wife Arati, then all the treatment will be done for free. Because he is an employee of the Steel Plant. The hospital takes money from the outsiders but everything is free for the staff members, even the medicines. Apart from it, if he does so, his weight will increase in front of his brother-in-law.

But Abhijeet opposed it. He said, "Brother! Why shall we resort to lies for the small expenses?"

But Adinath was stubborn. His arguement was, "many people are doing many injustices. Leaders, Ministers, Engineers, Businessmen are earning crores of rupees in dishonest way. What will be the harm if we, the common people, tell a little lie. You see! in the movie Seeta our Geeta, Rama or Shyam, no one could recognize the two people with the identical face. They could not know who is Seeta and who is Geeta, who is Rama and who is

Shyam. They have taken advantage of it. You know that in the Mahabharata, in the dance (Rasaleela) of Srikrishna, he used to dance with the company of sixteen thousand Gopis. All Gopis had a Srikrishna with them. In today's history, the great rulers like Germany's Adolf Hitler, Iraq's Saddam Hussein and Russia's Vladimir Putin, all Secretly keep duplicates, so that the plots to kill them can not succeed. Also, even when they are bedridden with disease they will carry out Government work through their duplicates. Even a book "The strange death of Adolf Hitler" published in 1939 stated that the real Hitler had been dead since 1938, but the duplicate was running the world war-II, Like that, let us take the advantage of Arati and Aditi's identical appearance.

Abhijit had nothing more to say. Aditi was admitted in the hospital under the name of Arati. They thought that this fever & cough was due to a slight cold. It may be due to new water and air or for a new place. Because the fever did not subside for three to four days and she vomited blood while coughing, various tests were conducted on her. But the doctors were not able know why these were happening. Gradually her health began to deteriorate. But the doctor assured that she would be fine. She will get well soon. As the saying goes, "God is like a rope and man is a cow, where He pulls there he goes". What people think, what they expect, they do not always get it. Sometimes they get opposite results. Here, that was what happened. After about fifteen days of treatment, Aditi (Arati) died suddenly one night. The doctor said, "She had a sudden heart attack". No one ever expected that.

It was like a lightning without cloud. Adinath's mind began to spin like a whirlwind. No doubt he had the grief of Aditi's death, but as far as everyone knew, it was Arati who died. Because, Aditi's treatment was done in the name of Arati, the doctor had also issued the death certificate in the name of Arati. What will he do now? He did not seem to find any way out from this situation. Gradually, the news of Arati's (Aditi's) death spread among his friends and colleagues in Rourkela. Some had telephoned to know the fact. Some others came to the hospital. Adinath felt that this lie could not be hidden for a long period. Because the friends can infer something from Arati and Abhijit's behavior. Then truth will come out. No! He has to do something.

On the other hand, the condition of Abhijit was bad. He never thought that only two years of married life would end so soon. He was completely devastated. He was not in a position to think about anything. He was sitting next to Aditi's dead body like a statue. What way he will show or what advice he will give.

Meanwhile, the doctor has given permission to take the dead body. Adinath's brain was working very rapidly. He was thinking that if the funeral rites will be done here then it will be in the name of Arati, which no one in the house can accept. If the dead soul truly gets peace and salvation by the funeral rites, then what will happen to Aditi's soul. The rituals will be performed in the name of Arati. Further, when the truth comes to the light then he will be entangled in fraud case. The police will come and arrest him. Then there may be departmental inquiry in the office. There may be trouble for his job. Oh God! What happened? Adinath was in despair.

Meanwhile Abhijit had come. He said, "Whatever happened has already happened. Now I will hire a vehicle and take the dead body to my place. Aditi's funeral rites will be held there."

But Adinath did not want it. Because, if Abhijit will

take away Aditi's dead body, then it will be clear that it was Aditi who was being treated in the hospital and not Arati. He said, "Look Abhijit! You know everything. The first priority now is to save my job. Therefore, I request you to take Aditi's dead body to her village i.e. our father-in-law's village instead of your place. I have informed our father-in-law everything. He must have arranged all the required things. In the meantime, I will think about what can be done. We have to leave this place before all my friends reach here. He called his father-in-law, Damodar babu.

Damodar babu already knew the matter from Arati. He gave his consent.

Adinath left the hospital. He has to reach home soon. He was thinking on the way, "I have to hire two vehicles. One vehicle will carry the dead body accompanied by someone. He will go in the other vehicle with his wife and two children.

After reaching home, he was surprised at the sight of Arati. As if her age has increased by ten years during this small period. Too much worry and sadness are the reasons for it. As soon as she saw him, Arati asked, tell me now who am I? Arati or Aditi? If any of your colleagues comes, then how will you introduce me?

Adinath answered, "Please Arati! Do not criticize me more. I agree, I have made a mistake, due to which the ambiance of sadness and discontent has been created in our two families today. I did not do this with any evil intention. It happens. Arati! Sometimes it happens. However, what has happened has already happened. Now please prepare yourself quickly. We have to leave this place as soon as possible. All the funeral rites will be done in your village. During this time we can think something.

At last everything proceeded accordingly. Adinath

requested the hospital authority and brought an ambulance on rent. Aditi's dead body and Abhijit went in it. Others took a taxi. The distance between Rourkela and Arati's village is about one hundred kilometers. It took around two hours to reach there. Damodar babu had organized everything. Amidst the mournful atmosphere, preparations began to take Aditi's mortal remains to the cremation ground. The last bed of man is the bier consisting of six pieces of bamboos. And final destination is the cremation ground where he rests in eternal sleep, having shed all the complication of this world. No one has been excluded from this process yet. He may be a king or beggar or a powerful politician, an emperor or a common man. Yes! Some are going on biers and some in coffins. Someone's dead body is being offered to the fire and someone is being buried under the ground. This is the eternal truth of man.

Aditi's body had been consumed by fire since a long time. The persons shouldering the dead body have returned after collecting her bones. Meanwhile Abhijit's parents have also arrived. The shock of Aditi's death and the tension of Adinath's mistake further complicated the atmosphere in the house. Everyone is sitting quietly. Nobody is talking. But Adinath's head is full of problems. There is no solution in sight. Aditi's purification rites will be done in the usual way. There is no problem in it. But the problem is in Adinath's office, the problem is in Arati's identity, the problem is in Abhhijit's future family life. What will he do?

Everyone in Rourkela and in his office knew that Arati is dead. So how will he take Arati to Rourkela? What he will say to his friends and relatives? He cannot stay without Arati. How can Arati live without him? And the matter of Abhijit! His wife is dead but still alive legally. How will he handle the one-year-old child? How can he get his wife's insurance policy money? Further, he has been married only for two years. A long life lies ahead of him. If he want to marry again, then how it will be possible? Oh! So many questions. The whole head is reeling.

All eyes are on Adinath. What will he say? He has created the problem. So he will have to solve the problem. Gradually everyone's silence was becoming unbearable. Finally Damodar babu broke the silence and spoke, "Now you say Adi! What shall we do? We have to proceed accordingly".

Adinath replied in a worried voice, "Baba! As my head was not working properly, I took a wrong decision which put the whole family in trouble. However, one thing comes to my mind. I have made a plan after a lot of thinking".

Everyone eagerly looked towards him. Adinath said, "According to the current medical certificate, Arati is dead. Offices and courts will accept it. That means, who is alive now is Aditi and she is Abhijit's wife. But in reality it is not true. Therefore, we have to amend it. Abhijit will divorce Aditi. If a couple, with mutual consent, apply to the court for divorce, it will be materialized quickly. Then after a few days, I will marry Aditi (actually Arati) and bring her home. Aditi's daughter will also come to us with her. Arati can take care of two children. Then all problems will be solved. If no one agrees to this, then let Arati stay here, in her father's house. I will come regularly. Because, in the current situation, there is danger if Arati will go to Rourkela.

Everyone was listening to Adinath. There was total silence in the room. It seemed from everybody's expression that both of his proposals were not acceptable. A sign of despair on each person's face. It was Damodar babu who finally opened his mouth, "What you are suggesting is not really possible. We have some respect in the society. Many people listen to us and obey us. What will they say? Can we hold our heads high anymore? This plot of divorce and marrying with you again are beyond our imagination."

Abhijit inquired, "If Aditi is alive then how will I get her insurance money? Arati, who had been sitting quietly and hearing all these things for so long, suddenly shouted. Everyone's eyes were drawn towards her. She retorted in an angry voice, "Your head has really gone mad, otherwise you would not have said such things". Then she softened her voice and said, "Look! All humans make mistakes. But when a noble person realizes that he has made a mistake, he tries to rectify it. Sometimes his pride prevents him. Therefore, he suppresses his ego and pride and goes all out to correct the mistake. Apart from it, I do not want to live the rest of my life as Aditi. I am Arati, and I will live as Arati. Can our society easily accept all these divorce, remarriage? We are all educated, polished and cultured people. If you have made a mistake, you should face it with courage. Then you will have your self-respect.

"Abhimanam Dhanam Jesan Chiram Jibanti te Narah, Abhiman Bihinanam Kim Anen Kamayusa."

It means that "Those who consider Abhiman (Self-respect) as wealth will indeed be eternal. People with low self-esteem have no value in their wealth or life."

So, maintain your self-respect. Go tomorrow and report the incident to your higher authority. Then accept the punishment given by them as penance. You are a highly qualified technician. This steel plant will not leave you easily. Because there are very few employees like you. They may give some punishment but cannot take away your job. And if the job is gone, then there are many opportunities in this world to fill our bellies. Everything will be fine. The medical certificate will be changed. Aditi will die in place of Arati. Abhijit will not have any problem in getting the insurance amount.

Every person was sitting quietly and listening to Arati's remarks, perhaps supported it. Suddenly Adinath got up from his seat and holding Arati's hands he said, "You are right. Aditi's death and my lying, wrong doing had disturbed my head. I could not find any way. You have opened my eyes. I will go to the office tomorrow and reveal all the truths". He felt a little relaxed.

***

"If you are not making mistakes, then you are not doing anything. I am positive that a doer makes mistakes." - John Wooden

Who Am I ?

By the time the train reached the station, it was already 10 A.M. Somanath quietly got down. A long twenty seven hours journey from Bhubaneswar to Bengaluru. Sitting on the train for so long is boring. He came out of the platform. He has to get a prepaid taxi. His son was ready to come to the station. But he refused. It is difficult to get out of his busy office work. He is also not new to Bengaluru. His son, Rosan, is working in Bengaluru. Wife Bimala often comes and stays with him for a few days. She has been here since a month. He has also come to spend a few days here and will return with Bimala. Rolling his trolley bag, he went to the prepaid taxi counter. There was a long line. He has to stand in the queue. Around twenty people were in front of him. Standing in the line he looked around. Meanwhile, it must have rained. It was completely wet weather. Suddenly his eyes fell on a group of people crowding at some distance. Something must have happened. Should he go there and see ? No... No..., his turn would come on this side. But he was anxious. He observed that his turn would come after sometime. Unable to suppress his curiosity, he beckoned to the man behind him to secure his place in the line and walked to that place.

When he reached, he saw an old man sitting there. Four or five days old beard was on his face. His dresses were of good quality but had become dirty. The people were asking him different questions in different languages. But he did not answer to anyone. Only looking at them blankly. Four to five people came out of the crowd and dragged him to take him away. Somanath did not understand anything. Who is this old man and who are they all, why are they dragging him ?

Suddenly the old man shouted, "who are you ? Where are you taking me ?" Hearing these words, Somanath could know that this person is an odia. But those who are trying to take him away are not odias. Why do they want to take him away ? Why is this old man not revealing his identity ?

A thought came to Somanth's mind. Is he a dementia patient? It is a disease that destroys a person's memory. He will not be able to know who he is, where he comes from and what he is doing. One of his friend's father had this disease. Once he had left home and was wandering around aimlessly. After a lot of searching he was traced. Has that happened in this case ? But why are these people forcefully pulling him. Doubts crossed his mind. Now a days there are frequent reports in the newspapers regarding the dubious transactions in human organs. People are selling the human organs like kidney, liver for a lot of money. Those people must have wanted to take him away for that purpose.

A thought struck to his mind. He called 100 from his mobile. He explained the police about the problem and requested them to come immediately. He also informed the exact location of the place. Generally, lower level employees do not understand Hindi or English, only Kannad. However somebody understood Hindi and they agreed to come.

Meanwhile, his turn at the taxi counter must have come. But he did not want to leave the old man in such a situation. Meantime, his son called him. He informed that he is with a friend and will be back after a while.

Those people were trying continuously to drag away the old man. He could not keep quiet anymore. He had already informed the police. He went and caught hold of the old man's hand and said, "Uncle ! where from did you flee?" He said in Hindi to those people, "he is my relation. He can not remember anything due his memory loss and ran away from house."

The old man held Somanath's hand and said, "who am I ? why are these people pulling me ?" Those four men stared at him, saying something in Kannada and trying to drag the old man again. Fortunately, the PCR van arrived at that time. All those people ran away. Somanath explained everything to the police and also said that he did not know him either. He could understand from his language that he is from his state. He wants to take the unknown old man to his real home.

As the police looked at him questioningly, he said, "I need a good voluntary organisation to help that person." He wished to take that old man to his home. But he feared that some legal complicacies may occur. Apart from that his wife and son may also be upset. But he can not be left like this. For that he felt the necessity of an NGO. As per the instruction of the police, he went to the police station along with the old man in the police vehicle.

After reaching the police station, he called his wife and told her that it would be a little late though he knew that she would have already known it from their son. Somanath had to wait there for some time. The police contacted an agency. They reached there after some time. After learning everything, they searched the old man's pant and shirt pockets, hoping to find some evidence.

At this time, Somanath's eyes fell on the sticker of a shop near the waist of the pant. He ran there and found out that it belongs to a tailoring shop in Brahmapur. So he assumed that this person is from Brahmapur.

Immediately, he called a friend at Brahmapur; told him the entire problem and requested him to publish a news in the local news paper regarding finding of a missing person. He took a photo of the old man on his mobile and sent it to his friend through whatsApp. He also told to contact him on his mobile number. He came back after leaving the old man in the care of the NGO and gave his phone number to contact him if needed.

He reached home by hiring an auto. He was very much tired due to long train journey as well as the trouble for the old man. He took his bath and finished his lunch. Wife Bimala wanted to ask something but kept silent looking at his tired face. He lay down on the bed. The old man's face was floating before his eyes. What would have happened to him today ? Anyway he had escaped. Who could be there in his family ? whether they were looking for him or not ? Has he been neglected? Taking advantage of his forgetfulness, they must have left him, not guarding properly. This is how the world has become. The people have become so selfish that they have lost their moral values.

Hey, no… no… why is he thinking like that ? Gradually he fell asleep.

In the evening his son returned from the office. After hearing everything he was disturbed. He knows his father. He can not tolerate seeing someone's problems. He goes out to help that person without thinking about his own difficulties and troubles. But is it okay to involve in those matters at this age? He said in a worried voice, "why were you involved in this trouble ? So many things are happening like this. Can we help everyone?" At that time, wife Bimala added, "I am tired of advising. But he is not listening."

Somanath looked at his son's face and said with a smile, "we can not do anything for everyone. But, what is the harm, if we can do something for some people within our limit ? I feel very happy that I have saved him from an imminent danger. I will feel peace when he unites with his family."

After three days, Somanath received a phone call. A gentle man from Brahmapur thanked him and said that he would be reaching Bengaluru very soon.

He got a call from the organisation and reached the police station. After a while, the organisation people arrived there with the old man. The old man looked better than that day and wore clean clothes. As soon as the gentle man from Brahmapur saw the old man, he embraced him and wept. He said, "what is this, father! You came like this. We have been searching for you. Let us go now."

At that time the old man said, "who are you, why are you crying ?" Again he said, "who am I ? where will you take me?"

While weeping, the gentle man said, "you are my father. Mother, your daughter-in-Law, grand son, grand daughter, all in the house are waiting for you."

Somanath could feel the helplessness of the gentle man. Such is the bond of love and affection in our country. A man is not neglected even if he gets old and when his necessity for the society is no more required. One who can serve his old parents feels blessed. The bond of love and affection we have in our family is uncomparable. Some people are forgetting their humanity and neglecting their duties. For that, perhaps for a moment such a thought entered in to his mind.

With tears in his eyes, the gentle man held the hands of Somanath and said, "I do not know how to thank you. I am surprised and also happy to think that there are persons like you in this world. Otherwise, this earth would not have survived. In today's world, inhumanity has increased so much that it is a pity to think of it. They do not understand anything except money. They forget their relationships for money. Even they do not hesitate to kill for it."

Somanath said to him that there is no need to thank him for this. I have done only a normal humanitarian work. By God's grace you have got your father back. It was your love, fondness and devotion that brought him back to you. Now you treat him and try to cure him sooner. As far as I know, this disease is not completely curable but you have to take medicines regularly. Apart from that, he has to be guarded at all times. Yes, if you want, you can stay at our house for a few days with your father. The gentle man said, "I have booked tickets in tomorrow's train. Please do not worry further."

Somanath said, "What is the problem? No problem at all. Please come. Today you both will stay at our house."

He came home with them. Next day, he booked an auto rikashaw and sent them to the railway station. After all, he was able to find out the identity of the old man and hand over him to his family. His mind was filled with self-satisfaction.

***

"I am who I am. Not who you think I am. Not who you want me to be. I am me." - Brigitte Nicole

The Shadow

The doctor announced his final verdict. There is no hope at all. No medicine, no injection is working any more. Perhaps within four to five days at any point of time the last moment may arrive. Surekha was sitting like a stone statue. There were no more tears in her eyes. As if, all the tears had exhausted. The doctor had left long ago. But Surekha was sitting as before.

How all these happened ? Every thing turned upside down only within ten days. She remembered that incident of ten days ago. Abinash suddenly fell down while delivering a speech in a teacher's gathering. He was rushed to a renowned hospital. The doctor examined and said, "brain stroke, surgery is needed immediately." The operation was also done. But nothing happened. As per doctor's advice, he was taken home after staying for three days in I.C.U. The doctor used to come and see him everyday. Liquid food was fed through a pipe. That has been also stopped since last two days. His body was no longer accepting anything. He was lying motionless. Only breathing slowly. On hearing the news, the sons and daughters-in-Law have come. Their elder son lives in Mumbai and the job of the younger one is at Hyderabad. The elder son has a son and the younger has a daughter. Abinash was a professor of economics. After retiring from the government job, he got a job in a private college. He was the leader of the Odisha School and College joint teacher's union. He became everyone's favorite due to his strong personality and integrity.

She and Abinash were from the same village. They both were born in lower middle class families. After passing matriculation from the same school, they were studying in the same college in a near-by town. Like many others, they were also commuting by bycyles. Meanwhile, they did not know when they were attracted to each other.

Surekha came to her senses at the call of Tanmay. For a moment, she had gone back to the distant past. She looked back. Her sons and daughters-in-Law were standing and requesting her to eat something and take rest. With this condition of Abinash, can she take any food or take rest? She has been sitting like that for the last two days, even she has not taken a drop of water. She said, "you all go, take care of your children, eat something and take rest. I am sitting here." Everyone left. But Tanmay Lay on the sofa kept there and said, "I am sleeping here. Please call me if necessary."

The ticking sound of the clock was continuing. Surekha was sitting as before. She was looking at Abinash's face with focused eyes. It was midnight. She held Abinash's hand with her both hands. As if the life-less hand shivered in the palm of her hands.

She felt that apparently Abinash could understand something. She pressed her hands a little more. A cold current flowed within her and she floated away in that current to her distant past. She dragged the chair nearer to the bed and brought her face close to Abinash's face and continued talking about their love story.

Do you remember, Abinash, the sweet evening of that day. We were sitting on the banks of the river. Clear autumn sky. You plucked a bunch of Kasatandi flowers (wild sugar cane or kans grass flower) from the river bed, knelt down before me and said, "I love you, Surekha. I can not live without you. Do you love me?" Do you recollect, what answer did I give to your question? You must have remembered. Yet I am repeating. Please listen. I replied, "I love you too. I am like your shadow, I will be with you wherever you go."

Further you asked, "But Surekha! The shadow vanishes in the darkness. Would you not leave me in the difficult days of my life?

I replied, "This is your misconception. The shadow never leaves. It is always there. Nothing can be seen in the dark. Not a single thing. Not even the person himself. But when illuminated, everything is visible including the shadow."

After passing B.A., my family was looking for a suitable candidate for me and you were searching for a job. Even if you wanted to study more, you were not able to do so because of the financial situation of your home. At that time, our family members heard about our love affair. Our parents were not much educated but they were well natured and cultured. Also god believer. They thought our love as God's grace and got us married. We moved to Bhubaneswar with limited resources to build our future. To live in Bhubaneswar was difficult, finding a house on rent was even more difficult. But by God's mercy, we got a house on Lesser rent and there we started our struggle for the existence in life. We had love for each other. There was affection, reverence and respect between us. It was decided between us that one will study and the other will do a job. You told me to read first. But I refused and said that, "I am looking for a job. You do your M.A. After your studies are over and after you get a job, then only I will think about my study." You did not agree with me. I was forcing. There were arguments between us. Finally, it was resolved that I will do the job. Luckily I got a job in a private school. You took admission in Vani Vihar. My Low salary from the private school was not sufficient to pay our house rent, your college fees and our running household expenses. So, in the evening I tutored some children at home. Even though it was difficult, but my heart was filled with joy. On some days we used to eat flattened rice or fried rice as dinner. There was no remorse at all. Over the time your M.A. course was completed. You passed with very good marks. There was not much competition then. So you got a Lecturer job due to your good marks. After receiving first month's salary, you compelled me to resign from my job and get admission in M.A. course. I did not want to study anymore. But I read only to keep your words and also passed with good marks. Since English was my subject, I also got a job as a lecturer in a local private college. After a long struggle, we breathed a sigh of relief. Our marital life grew sweeter. After a year, Tanmay came to our life. Mother-in-Law came, stayed with us and took the responsibilities of the child. After two years another son was born. It was you who named him as Chinmay. Our life become colorful and lyrical. The days were passing smoothly. Both the children were growing up. Despite the presence of mother-in-Law, I had to work hard. I was still happy to do household works, children's works along with my official works. It was not difficult at all. The affection, love and understanding between us made the course of our life easy and beautiful. It was a pleasant experience of married life. You became a leader of the teachers. Your admiration and respect increased all around.

Not that there was no storm in our married life. But we braved the storm and solved the problems. Do you remember? That time you went to Kolkota to attend the conference of the All India teacher's Association. Here the Government was infuriated on you. Because you were the leader of All Odisha School College joint teachers and employees union. You were fighting to abolish the block grant system in Odisha which did not exist in any other state in India. The lecturers under the Block Grant Scheme were paid much less salary than their counter parts which is contrary to the supreme court order, "equal work, equal pay."

The entire Odisha teacher's society was waiting for your return. The campaigning will begin after your arrival. Meanwhile an obscene C. D. went viral on all mobiles. In that C.D., it was seen that you were with a girl in a room. Although the girl's face was not clearly visible, your face was fully visible. It came to my mobile too. The next day it was published in all the news papers, "the black deed of the teacher's Leader."

You know, I did not believe it even for a second. I called you immediately. You were trying to prove your innocence. I said. "I do not need any explanation. I know, what you are. You can never do such a low and despicable thing. I am behind you, just like a shadow." Then I called a press conference and said, "I have known Abinash since childhood. I also know what his character is. Human character does not change overnight. There is no doubt that this C.D. is a hoax. It should be investigated. The C.D. should be sent to the Laboratory for testing. The police should investigate the matter and arrest the real culprit and make arrangements to punish him. I will go on indefinite hunger strike in front of the collector's office if the culprit is not caught within seven days". The entire Odisha teacher community were behind us. You know that within seven days the cyber police managed to catch the person who prepared such a C.D. by doctoring the girl's photo with your photo.

Then again the wheel of our family life rolled on. There were differences, misunderstandings, arguments between us. But they were all momentary. There was an unwritten rule between us. When one is angry, the other will be silent. So things did not ever escalate. Everything was going well.

Both sons got married. Both the daughters-in-Law are very good. We always wanted the best for everyone. Never think bad of anyone. May be, that's why our sons and daughters-in-Law are so good. They are full of respect, devotion and love for us. You always used to say, God helps those who do good to others and help others. I always agree with you.

Truly, our family seems like a heaven to me. From every aspect, we have a complete family. We spent our retired life happily. We played with our grand children. What else do we need. You are already seventy five years old. I am also close to it too. No disease has ever touched us. We never required any medicine. There is no more desire in our life.

Surekha paused a little. She took a deep breath and looked at Abinash more closely. She examined by putting her hand under his nose. The breathing was becoming slower.

She pressed his hand even harder by her palms and continued again. "Can you hear me? Sure, you can. Are you scared? Do not be afraid of. You know what was Yaksha's last question to Yudhisthir in Mahabharat."

"What is the most surprising thing on earth?"

Yudhisthir's answer was, "man knows that death is inevitable. Death is real. But he is doing such works, as if he will not die. He will live for ever." Death is certain. But the soul does not die. The soul is immortal.

It is written in the Geeta that,

"Nainm Chhindati Sastrani, Nainm dahati Pabakah;

Na chaina Kledayanti Apo na Sosayati Maruta."

That means, "No weapon can cut the soul. Fire can not burn it. Water can not moisten and the wind can not dry it."

So you have nothing to fear. We came to this world separately. But we will go together. Savitri brought back her husband Satyaban from the clutches of Yama. But I can not do that. But I can not stay without you. Because I am your shadow. I will be by your side always.

The eye lids of Surekha were closing gradually. She became very weak due to not taking any food or drink, along with mental agony. Her legs and hands were slowly and surely becoming motionless. Still trying somehow, she looked at Abinash. His fading breath has stopped.

Abinash … with a faint scream, she fell on Abinash's motionless body.

Even though Tanmay was pretending to sleep on the sofa, there was no sleep in his eyes. He was listening to the love story of his parents. The sweetness of their marital life. He came running after hearing the scream of his mother. He shook his mother in panic.

But it was all over. Two soul birds already flew away. Only the mortal remains of the two bodies were lying there. He started screaming loudly.

***

(This story was published in "Sudhanya", in their "Couple special issue" in January 2018.)

"Love that ends is the shadow of Love, true love is without beginning or end." - Hazrat Imayat Khan

The Lockdown

Sometimes a person falls into such a precarious situation, which he never dreamed of. Who ever thought that an invisible virus like corona will come and create a mayhem of terror all over the world and will change all the rules and regulation of the society. What will he do now? Saswat could not see any way out. After a long time, he came to his father-in-Law's house in Rayagada with his wife Sarika and six-year-old son. Father-in-Law was not well. Apart from it, Sarika had not gone to her father's house since a long period. That is why they came to Rayagada for fifteen days. He had already booked the train tickets earlier. The return tickets were also booked. They came on 15th March. They were to return on twenty eighth. But the Lockdown for carona caused all the chaos. The Prime Minister announced a Lockdown from 25th March to April 14th. The movement of trains, buses, taxis were stopped. The offices, markets, malls and factories were all closed: All were prohibited to leave the house without a valid reason. You could go outside only for essential commodities like groceries, vegetables or medicines.

Saswat had no problem for himself. His company had allowed him to work from home. So it did not matter whether he was in Bhubaneswar or in Rayagada. Only worriness was for his parents. His father is seventy years old and mother is sixty five years old. Now the corona is a big danger for them. How they will manage, he can not think of. They came only for fifteen days. Accordingly he had kept all the essentials for them. But now everything has gone upset. The return path is blocked. Father has blood pressure, diabetes and mother has diabetes and waist pain too. What they will do when the medicines will run out? Father has no A.T.M. So there is no sense in sending money on line. He can not draw it. It was never needed in the past.

The Lockdown till 14th April was extended again till 3rd May. He was talking with his father, Akhil babu. The ration was almost over. They did not have much money with them. Further, he himself can not go out anywhere. Saswat assured him and said, "do not worry. I will see what can be done."

He said it but what could he do? Saswat was very much worried. Seeing his anxiousness Sarika said, "you have so many friends. Tell someone to give some money and other necessary articles at our house. We will repay it when we will return."

Saswat liked the idea. He contacted a friend on mobile and requested to help him.

The friend's voice floated from the other end, "we are completely trapped : our entire colony has been declared as containment zone. We can not go anywhere and no one can come to our place. The situation will be reviewed again after fourteen days."

He called another friend. But there also the response was hopeless. "There is very little cash at home. We have difficulties in maintaining our house. We are also afraid of withdrawing money from A.T.M. There is more chances of contagion from the A.T.M.s"

Another friend told, "ours is a red zone. There are many restrictions. So the question of going anywhere does not arise."

This is indeed the time of trouble for everyone. Nobody can do anything for anybody. Still Saswat called another friend.

The friend replied, "Now the police is beating anybody going outside without a valid reason. Therefore, for fear of beating, I do not leave the house."

Saswat realised that no one has the attitude to help. If someone wanted, he could find a way and do something. One friend said directly, "you are enjoying your stay at your father-in-Law's house and putting us in trouble." Ofcourse, he said it jokingly. Leave it.

Now a days finding a good friend is very difficult. Whoever has one true friend is really lucky. It is not friendship that comes with a smile in good times but the one who stands beside you in times of danger is a true friend. This is the age of selfishness. Everyone wants their comfort and happiness, reluctant to spend a little time or Labour for others. To expect all these is in vain.

After hearing negatively from his friends, Saswat thought whether he should call their neighbourer Mishra uncle. But they are not in talking terms since two years. He has constructed the boundary wall on our land and started building an asbestos house on it. There was a quarrel due to the protest of his father. Strange man! They will deviate all rules to construct a house. They will not leave even an inch from their land but encroach the neighbourer's land and construct house on it. Measurement of plots were conducted due to complain of his father. Since that day, two families were not in talking terms. So what kind of help he could do? Saswat could not think of any other way.

Should he call the police? A helpless old couple is in trouble. But what will the police do? Their days are passing in controlling the unruly people.

He remembered Surath, who is staying in the tin house in their backyard. He is a daily Labourer. It is not known how they have managed their family as all the works have stopped. Where self survival is impossible, what help he will give? Still, as a last resort, he called him. But did not succeed. It must have been an old mobile and not working properly. Saswat was completely disappointed. When a man is helpless, he turns to God. Not finding any way, he prostrated before god and prayed, "Lord show me some way. You have heard the prayer of Draupadi and saved her by providing crores of clothes in the Kuru royal court. You can help me if you want."

The Meteorological Department has announced, "strong winds and rain are likely to occur in some districts including Khorda from tonight." Ketaki was disturbed. Now this worsening situation is prevailing due to the outbreak of corona. To add fuel to fire, this information of rain and storm. Surath was not feeling well. She had to go, bring necessary things. It will continue to rain for two to three days. It is already 11AM. She quickly finished cooking and went to the nearby shop. While closing the front gate, she saw aunty sitting on a plastic chair on the outside veranda. She had not been to their house for almost twenty days due to the Lockdown. Aunty was the one who refused her to come. She is seeing her after a long period. She was looking very weak. She came back from the gate and asked her, "do you need anything? I will bring it. I am going to the shop."

"No, what you will bring for me. We do not need anything." Aunty said. After observing her gloomy face and trembling voice, Ketaki enquired, "aunty! Are you not feeling well?"

The human mind is very weak and fragile. When someone speaks affectionately at the time of trouble, tears flow from the eyes automatically. Hearing the kind words of Ketaki, tears rolled from her eyes. She cried like a child.

Ketaki asked worriedly, "is everything alright, aunty? Are brother and the kids okay?"

What could go right! They stayed on that side and we on this side. They were to come back after fifteen days. Accordingly they have kept the necessary things for us. Now this Lockdown is getting extended time and again. Everything we have are finished. We can not contact him on phone. We are in trouble. Our son must be very much worried there. There is not much work here. Everyone is asked to stay at home due to the fear of corona. That's why I refused you to come. We have not cooked for the last two days. No rice, no pulses. We do not even have money. Our son was saying that some how he would send money for us. But nothing has materialised. Uncle called a friend of him who lives in this town. Unfortunately for us, he has been infected with corona virus. Now he is in the hospital. All his family members are in quarantine. Being hopeless from everyside, the only thing left is to pray God.

Yesterday, we ate a handful of ukhuda (fried rice mixed with molasses) kept as an offering for God and drank water. Since this morning we have not eaten a single grain. Only drank some water. We have also run out of medicines. We can not even make contact with our son. Tears were flowing from her eyes.

Ketaki did not feel like going to the shop. She sat there at a distance and said, "I was not able to know anything as I was not coming to your house. Because of this awful disease all movements were stopped. You were so much in trouble but you did not tell us anything."

Hey! What can you do? Your condition must be unbearable. Surath must not be able to go to work.

We are fine, aunty. Do not worry about us. Let me come from the shop. I will prepare and bring some food for you both. Is uncle okay?

Yes, He is sleeping now.

Ketaki got up and left. After some time Ketaki and Surath came with food. The faces of both of them were covered with the towels. Putting the food and water jug in the corner of the veranda, Ketaki said, "this jug has water mixed with sugar and salt. Because your stomach is empty, first you will drink, then only you will eat."

After their departure, aunty was thinking, really how helpful and responsible they were. In the evening Surath brought bread and curry. He kept the food inside the house by stretching his hand from the veranda and sat in the corner of that veranda. Uncle and aunty were sitting on chairs. Uncle told, "what a situation. Lockdown continue to extend. How will the people live. The government is taking care of only poor people. They have given rice, pulses in advance for four months. Rich people have no problem. They buy everything online and stay comfortably. Only the middle-class people are in trouble. It hurts much to buy things at such high prices within their limited income. In spite of all the odds, we could have managed if our son were with us. Unfortunately for us, our children have moved out at this juncture."

Surath said, "uncle! If you do not mind I will tell something."

Akhil babu replied, "so many years of relationship with you. What shall I think? Speak what you want to speak."

Surath said, "the matter of fact is, you have said now that the government is providing advance ration to the poor people. As I have a B.P.L. card, I have also received advance ration. Now I have around sixty kilos of rice. You need not worry. I will give you some of it and I will bring the necessary vegetables and other things from the near by shops. It will be sufficient until your son comes. Also please give me the list of medicines, I will go and get them."

Akhil babu looked at his face with amazement. How kind and caring the poor man whom he had brought and kept in his backyard house. Actually, the heart of the poor is more generous than the heart of the rich. The rich is great only in wealth but the poor is great in mind and heart.

Surath wondered, "why are you looking to me like this? You are giving me for the last fifteen years. Because of your grace, I am able to stay in a place like Bhubaneswar. My voter card, B.P.L. card and Adhar card all are done here only. I have created an identity of my own here. Today I have got an opportunity to do something for you. Please do not refuse. I would be happy if I could help you in this difficult situation. I will consider myself blessed."

Surath had left the place. After some time he came with rice, pulses, oil, vegetables etc and kept them there.

Akhil babu was sitting quietly as before and thinking about Surath. It has been fifteen years since this house was built, he is staying in that backyard tin house. He brought him form a slum and kept him in that tin house to supervise his house construction work. He is a daily Labourer but very faithful. After they stayed in the house, his wife, Ketaki usually washes their dishes and cleans the house. Both are very good persons. And due to this corona, he was able to know how big is their heart and how pure is their mind.

This is true that the entire world is shaking in fear due to the hazards of corona. How much damage, how much trouble and how many people lost their lives. But if you will examine thoroughly, the wrath of corona is only for humans. As if it is created to destroy the men's anti-nature activities, pride and ego. It is the fountain of compassion for all except humans. The atmosphere is cleaner, the environment is free from pollution and the animals and birds are roaming happily. The trees and vines are all greener and looking beautiful. And how many lives have been lost due to corona? In the year 2018, more than one and half lakhs people died in road accidents. About two and half lakhs people die every year due to alcoholism. Compared to that, how many people has been killed by corona? He was analysing in his mind. Perhaps he was consoling himself.

Again Lockdown extended from 4th May to 17th May. Ofcourse, some relaxations has been made. There has been heavy rain and strong wind in Bhubaneswar for the last three days. Now it is raining even though there is no wind. There is no electricity also. The mobile phones are not working as the mobile towers are damaged. He was not able to make any contact with his father. Saswat could not bear it anymore. He has to go to Bhubaneswar by any means. He arranged a pass from the district authorities. He hired a taxi and left for Bhubaneswar. Sarika and his son stayed behind. They will come later. He has to stay in quarantine for fourteen days in Bhubaneswar at his father's house. And Rayagada is now in the green zone. Fully safe. The taxi was running in full speed. It will take about ten hours to reach Bhubaneswar. His unsteady mind was heaving with fear. How will be his parents? No phone call was possible for a long time. He could not get any information. It was five in the evening by the time he reached Bhubaneswar. He got out of the taxi and hurriedly entered the gate.

Both father and mother were sitting on the chairs. Sitting on the ground at a distance, Ketaki was talking with them. Parents were looking very fresh. Anyway, they seemed to be alright. So many thoughts were circulating in his mind. But this Ketaki was stopped to come to their home after the Lockdown. Because, there is fear of infection if someone from outside enters the house. Ofcourse, she was sitting at a safe distance on the outside veranda. She also put on a mask on her face. As soon as she saw him, she paid respect and departed. The faces of his parents lit up with happiness. Father asked, "Are you alone?"

Everyone is fine. I will tell everything. But tell me, how are you all? How much difficulty you must have faced. Observing the worriness of Saswat, Akhil babu said, "No. No. Nothing to worry. We did not know that there is such a huge piece of gold lying behind our house. For that we were a little disturbed. All is well now."

Saswat stared at his face without understanding anything.

Akhil babu told Saswat briefly about Surath and Ketaki and told him, "go and take a bath."

Saswat cautioned, "for the time being, you will stay away from me. I have to stay separately for fourteen days."

Saswat was thinking while entering the room, "in fact an ordinary man can not understand, when god helps whom and in which way". He folded his hands in reverence to God.

***

(This story was published in "Suddhanya" in their "corona special issue" in August 2020.)
"This pandemic has magnified every existing inequality in our society – Like systemic racism, gender inequality and poverty."
- Melinda Gates

The Stream Of Life

Even though she had woken up from her sleep, she was still lying on the bed. She decided not to go to her office today. So there is no hurry. It is okay if she will get up after half an hour. But she got up after a little while, Prepared tea for herself. She opened the window and looked outside. The streets were wet due to incessant rain. At that time her mobile rang. Dad called. Dad calls her almost every morning to wish good morning. She answered the phone, wished good morning and kept talking for a while.

Her father was a colonel in the Indian army. Now after retirement, he has been staying in the village for most of the time. He likes village life very much. And mother... No one knows her likes and dislikes. She continues to agree to every decision of father. They have a house in Bhubaneswar. A flat in an apartment. Dad does not like that apartment house at all. There is no area exposed to soil. He is a plant lover. That's why he spends his time in the village doing gardening and farming. He takes pictures of vegetable saplings, flower plants and send them to her on whatsApp. His hand-crafted garden is truly beautiful. She has not gone to her village since a long period. Earlier she used to go to her village almost in every vacation. Her village, surrounded by paddy fields, forests and a river is very beauteous. Ever since she went to Kolkata for a management course, she has not been able to go to the village. After passing out from there, she got a job in a company in Bengaluru. It has now been five years since she stayed here in Bengaluru. There is a lot of work pressure in the company job. Ofcourse she is getting a fat salary. But is this a life? Earn money, get married, have family, have kids-Is the life limited only to this much? There may be other aspects of life. She wants to do something for the society and live a meaningful life.

Since a few days, a thought has been circulating in her mind. She is getting restless. At times she can not function properly even in the office. Ever since her dad stayed in the village, the call of the village has been ringing in her ears. She can feel the smell of the village soil, even though she is in Bengaluru. Can she go and do something for the people of the village? Can she fill their dark lives with glorious lights?

It was too late. She went and finished her daily routine. Prepare food for her self. However, her mind was anxious as before. After thinking a lot, she came to a conclusion. But she has to inform Sumant about her decision. After all he is going to be her husband in near future.

Evening was fast approaching. The rain was falling as drizzle continuously. She called Sumant and talked about having dinner in a hotel.

Sumanta's voice from the other side... "Wow... what an idea! Dinner with you on such an evening is very romantic. I will leave the office in a little while. After reaching home, I will freshen up and go out immediately. However, it will be almost eight O'clock."

After passing engineering from I.I.T., Kharagpur, Sumant is serving in a top position in a multi national company. Strong personality, handsome figure. The only son of a rich family. The marriage of both of them has been finalized. So they usually go for outing without any hesitation. They go to hotel, watch cinema and also go for marketing.

But today, she has called him to tell an urgent matter. She does not know how Sumant will react after hearing her decision. But she took this decision after much deliberations. And she was pretty sure that she would not deviate from this decision.

She booked seats in a hotel in Koramangala on line and texted the hotel name to Sumant. She booked an ola cab and went to the hotel. She had to reach there before Sumant's arrival. She reached the hotel and waited for Sumant. Meanwhile, she ordered soup and starter. Sumant also arrived there very quickly.

As soon as he arrived, Sumant started teasing her. He said in a low voice, "this sudden dinner program indicates, madam is in a very romantic mood. To sit together and have dinner in this rain soaked evening of the first part of the month of July! Well, I have to appreciate your idea. "He started saying something more but stopped when he saw the serious face of Sampurna.

"What happened ? Any problem? Why so much tension?" Sumant was worried.

The soup and starter had arrived. While eating Sampurna said, "I have called you to tell something urgent."

"You could have said that on the phone. Are you kidding?" Sumanta remarked.

"No Sumant! I am not joking at all." Sampurna told in the same serious tone. "Well, please tell me, what is the value of this life and what is the goal of this life?"

"Oh! This is the matter. What is the goal? I do not know anybody's life. But as far as we are concerned-we both have good jobs. Earning Lakhs of rupees every month. After our marriage, we will go for a honeymoon to Switzerland. Then we will make a good home, give quality education to our children, spend our time in comfort and enjoy our life to the fullest. We will live long by eating nutritious foods." Sumant explained.

"Well! Is the aim of life limited to this much only? We, means you, me and our children, will live well and maintain a luxurious life. A Successful life is not to live a long life but a meaningful life. You are seeing only one side of the world through the coloured glass, Sumant. When you will look to the other side of the world, you will see, how the people are suffering for a drop of water, how a mother is selling her child for a small amount of money only to satiate her hunger. How have they lived their lives? It hurts to think."

Sumant's head was spinning after hearing this philosophical version of Sampurna. What a sudden transformation!

He flipped the menu without saying anything. He asked what to order.

Sampurna replied indifferently, "order your favourite to day."

The hotel boy took the order and left.

Sampurna said, "you know! I thought, I would leave this job and go to my village."

"What ! Are you joking with me? You will quit such an attractive job, leave such a big city and go to the village. Are you mad?"

No Sumant! I am serious. One of my friends who got married less than a month ago texted me that, there is no water in about 20 to 25 villages near my village. The women have to travel a long distance to fetch water. Wood mafias are cutting trees from the village forests. The heat is unbearable. Dad was also telling the samething. I think, I will go and do something. If I can do something for the suffering people, if I can put a smile on their faces, then I will know that this life is fruitful and blessed. My heart will be filled with joy.

A shadow of despair was visible in Sumant's eyes. He came with so much expectations. But all the hopes and dreams are vanished. The romantic evening has faded completely. He said "why did this strange thought enter into your head? There is a government to understand the problems of the people. You manage your matter. Please change your decision and start eating happily." Then Sumant started serving with his own hands.

While taking food, Sampurna explained, "I have chosen this path after much contemplation. There is no going back now. You know, father is now staying in the village, I will go there."

"What about me?" Desperation in the voice of Sumant. "Will you leave me? Our marriage has already been fixed. Meanwhile we have come closer. Can you forget all these?"

"Why should I leave you? You are always in my heart. I have accepted you as my husband. You are mine. Even if there will be a distance between us, you will remain in my heart. Although, the elephant is in the forest, it belongs to the king. Yes, if you will forget me or will accept any one else, then I will not say anything."

The meal was over. They came back. After dropping Sampurna, Sumant went on his way.

Indeed, Sampurna resigned. She called her father and informed him of her decision.

On that day both of them were sitting closely at the railway station. Sumant's face was teary.

Sampurna consoled, "why are you so worried? I am going with some good objectives. I will come back to your life when my aim is fulfilled. Ofcourse, if you want. If you decide to marry someone else and live happily, then I have nothing to say.

Sumant returned after Sampurna boarded the train. It was about one and half days journey. Then she had to take a taxi.

However, she arrived safely. Her father was very happy and he appreciated her decision. He told her, "you have done a good thing by coming here. Now we will do something together."

Sampurna learned many things from her father. She mixed with the people and understood their problems. Then only she started her work. As per her opinion, forest degradation must be prevented first. And its perimeter has to be increased by planting new trees. Therefore, awareness should be infused in to the minds of the people. Then only the people of twenty/ twenty five villages can escape from water scarcity and hot Summer. Women's committees were formed in every village. Incidentally, the panchayat election was scheduled to be held after six months and she was unanimously elected as Sarpanch.

A meeting of all women's associations was called. In her introductory speech, Sampurna said, "we have to stop the wood mafias from cutting the trees and new trees have to be planted. I am suggesting a proposal that every household will plant atleast ten trees and take care of them. The panchayat will provide the necessary funds. And in our villages, each girl will marry to a tree and a plaque with the name of the girl will be hung on that tree and red clothes with bangles also will be tied around the trees. Then one will Surely hesitate to cut down that tree. An old lady who was sitting in the meeting protested and said, "what are you talking about? Why should the girls will marry the trees? The villages as well as the girls will be disgraced."

In an effort to explain her, she said, "this is nothing new, aunty. There are many such examples. You must have read Mahabharat and you must understand it also. In Mahabharat Gandhari first married to a Sahada tree. Then only she married to Dhritarastra. Leave that matter. There are similar instances in the morden age too. There is a rumor that a famous girl also married to a tree before her marriage. Do you know who is she? She is Aisharya Ray, the miss universe and bollywood heroine. Before marrying Amitabh Bachchan's son Abhisek Bachchan, she married trees not once but twice. First she married to a peeple tree in Banaras and then to a Banana tree in Bengaluru.

The aunty understood the matter and sat down. Everyone supported Sampurna and gave her a big applause.

The work proceeded accordingly. The forest shook with drum beatings and hulahulis (a noise by women made by their tounges). The salukana (red clothes) and bangles were tied to each tree. The forest was crowded by the celebration of Jantal by each village in different days. (Jantal means the feast of villagers in the forest.)

Another idea struck Sampurna's mind. If a semi-circular dam could be built some where below the mountain, near the forest, then the rain water from the hill during the rainy season could be collected there. As a result the water in the wells and ponds in the villages would no longer dry up. By her efforts, the local M.L.A. and M.P. sanctioned money from their funds and the construction work started. As a result, within a year, a strong dam was built and became a huge reservoir.

There after the status of the villages changed dramatically. Due to the growth of forests, the atmosphere was no longer warm. Due to the availability of water, people could grow two crops in a year and improve their standard of living. All the people praised Sampurna whole heartedly. Dad's happiness knew no bounds. His chest swelled with pride. The Chief Minister also came to the village. After observing and hearing everything, he praised her and made a promise that she will contest as M.L.A. in the next election from his party.

In spite of all these, she used to call Sumant at regular intervals. So did Sumant. Both inquired about each other's well-being. Sumant always said the same thing, "you come back. Without you nothing is good here." For a moment the feelings of Sampurna got perturbed. She also wanted Sumant to be with her. But what could she do? She has to go forward on the path on which she has stepped in. Now she wants to extend her work to other areas, not limiting these twenty/ twenty five villages.

That was a moonlit evening in the month of October. Sampurna was sitting and deeply thinking about her upcoming works. She opened the front door at the sudden knocking sound. What is she seeing? She could not believe her eyes. Sumant was standing in front of her.

"You! You are here." The surprised voice of Sampurna.

Sumant explained, "I could not stay anymore. I thought a lot and atlast resigned. Without informing anything, I came suddenly only to surprise you. I also want to be associated with the stream of life you have adopted and to the new path you have stepped in. Together we will lead the new path and build a green earth."

The colonel was standing there. He said, "only if the concept of the people change, then the world will also change and the earth will become greener and prettier."

***

"Life, like a stream of water, is renewed and renewed.... Though it wears the appearance of continuity in form." - Rumi

The Deorbited Comet

Through the glass of the window, the moon light illuminates the house. Perhaps it is a full moon night. The moon-lit night sky must be looking very bright. But Kabita is lying on the bed with the doors and windows of the house closed and the lights turned off. She is looking only at the rotating fan above. Will she open the window and take a look? No … what more can she get from this moon light. Her life is filled with deep darkness. Of course, she herself is responsible for it. Knowingly she pushed her life into the fathomless depths of darkness. Even she did not think twice. Why she will blame anyone else when she had struck her leg herself with an axe. Whether it is light or darkness outside, she has nothing to do with it.

Many moon-lit nights, many dreams, all are lost. Why had she done such a mistake? She is not a stupid. She could not think a little or could not judge properly. By the influence of others, she had destroyed her already settled life. Did she not have her own wisdom or conscience? The mind of Kabita is very much disturbed today. Remembering the past things makes her feel ill at ease.

She is the daughter of a family living in a slum. Their family consists of her father, mother, two sisters and a brother. Mother works at other households and runs their home. Father is a daily Labourer. Whatever he earns, squanders in drinking. She was studying very well. She had a desire to study more. But after passing matriculation, she had no money to study in a college. But she was determined. If there is a will, there will be a way. A known person of her mother had arranged Pramod babu's house as an engagement for her. There she will cook in the morning and evening. She thought that she could attain college during the day time even after cooking both the times. She agreed.

The family of Pramod babu comprises of his wife and a son. His wife lost her eye sight due to some disease. One leg of Sudhir, his only son, is affected by polio. He has to take the support of crutches to walk. He also got a job in the bank under disabled quota. Kabita does all the small chores of the house along with cooking. Pleased with her work, Pramod babu bought a bicycle for her. He had also given her a mobile. Everyone liked her cooking. Sudhir is very calm and quite in nature. But he was attracted towards Kabita by her activities and behaviour. While complimenting her cooking, he started praising her looks as well. And one day he told his mother his heart. Pramod babu was angry as soon as he heard it. Anyway, they are a well to do family. His son is in a banking job. He did not agree to accept a house maid as his daughter-in-law. But at last, he agreed after much persuasion by his wife Gayatri Devi. Gayatri Devi said that her son's leg is affected by polio. It is doubtful whether a girl from a good family will be available for him or not. What is the problem if he is willing here. The girl is beautiful and educated. Her behaviour is also well cultured. Because of her poor background, she will hear and obey our instructions. At last Pramod babu consented and went to Kabita's house with the proposal.

No one in Kabita's house could believe it. The son of such a rich family wants to marry the maid servant and the parents are also consenting to it. But when Pramod babu told them the deficiency of his son, they were upset. They did not want to give their beautiful and educated daughter in the hands of a deformed person. Pramod babu could read their minds. He explained, "Look! My son is doing a bank job. Your daughter will live very happily. I came here because my son wants this. He is our only son. We do not want to break his heart. We will also help your family if necessary."

They were happy after hearing all these things. But Kabita! could she be happy? She never thought of it. A girl usually desires a handsome, healthy man as her husband. Can she be happy by marrying a disabled man? At this time, Nabin is not there. Nabin is a youth of their slum. He is driving an auto-rikshaw and earning well. There was a good friendship between her and Nabin. Kabita observed that Nabin wanted to speak something to her which he tried desperately. But he has not been seen for the last six months. Some say he has gone to village and some say he had gone to the big city to earn more. However, she felt very helpless. She contemplated that she will not shatter the happiness of her family. She will not destroy the castle of their hope. Her one decision may change the fortune of her family. He may be a polio patient but he has a good job and well-established family. Again, everyone loves her. Everything is fine. Ultimately, she agreed.

Everything was arranged properly. The marriage was performed on an auspicious moment. Many people commented many things. But no one listened to them. The girl came as daughter-in-law. The same house, same persons but she will live in a new role in that house. From the beginning, she took all the responsibilities. Everyone in the house loved her very much. She became the mother of a son after one year. The happiness of the house increased even more. Of course, the desire to study further remained unfulfilled. What is there in it? She lived well, stayed happily: what else did she need? Her friends come to visit her from time to time. She tries to send them off on the pretext of some work. They express their resentment for it. Some say that the slum girl married by trapping the boy. She does not listen to these things. She has her duties and responsibilities. She does her household works mindfully and tries to please everyone.

If human life is moving on easy, simple, and right path, then no one would have any problem. But the vicious circle of time does not allow that to happen. No one can tell when the course of one's life will suddenly change. That is what happened in Kabita's life. One day, while returning from the temple, she met Nabin. She observed that Nabin is looking very healthy and handsome. He is now driving a car instead of auto-rickshaw. He also bought a car. After meeting each other several times, it was Nabin who raised the issue. He loves Kabita very much. He could not convey it though tried many times. Meanwhile, he has moved to a big city and has been able to earn more. In the course of conversation, he started filling poison in the mind of Kabita. He persuaded her to leave the lame man. At first, Kabita was feeling bad for this type of talking. But after listening the same thing again and again, her mind began to change. Everything seemed pale in front of Nabin's handsome face. She was totally influenced by his sweet words.

Gradually, there was a change in her attitude towards the members of the family. She started neglecting and misbehaving with everybody. On some days she did not cook and ordered food from outside.

Even she gave stale and left over food to her father-in-law and mother-in-law. After learning all this Sudhir tried to make her understand the matter. But she was not in a position to understand anything. Rather she retorted, "I am tired of doing things for the patients of this house. I cannot do it anymore."

Sudhir looked at her with surprise. Perhaps, he was thinking, "Is this the same Kabita whose words were dropping with honey and whose activities made this house happy?" How a human mind can change like this. He also got angry and told her some words angrily. Irritated by this, she came back to her parent's house. She felt like a free bird in the open sky. She mixed with Nabin and roamed with him at her will. Her parents tried to explain a lot to her. They advised her not to proceed on such a disagreeable path. But Satan had already captured her. Why should she listen to anyone? And one day, on the advice of Nabin, she lodged a case in the police station for domestic violence and dowry harassment. As a result, Sudhir and his parents were taken to the police station. Our law is such that only a girl's words are believed. No matter what Sudhir said in the police station, the police were not ready to listen to him. They were compelled to compromise and agreed to give whatever she demanded. But they requested her to return their grandson. But she refused. Finally, in the presence of lawyers, an agreement was reached. Kabita received one-time lump sum compensation. With it, she also got more money for the maintenance of her son. She also took many things from Sudhir's house, claiming that she had brought them at time of her marriage. Although she did not bring a penny. Pramod babu agreed to everything. Because he did not want to enter in to any court or police litigation. At last, both of them signed the divorce document. There was an end of a chapter.

Kabita became very happy after the divorce. There

were no more obstacles. She started weaving the net of imagination of the life with Nabin. They were roaming at their will without caring anything. Her parents could not bear it and drove her out of the house. Then, she stayed in a rented house with Nabin. A large amount of money has been deposited in her name in the bank. She started living a happy life with Nabin. But she was unable to know that the pieces of bricks were falling from the building of the world of her happiness.

Whenever she raised the matter of marriage, Nabin used to postpone it. He elucidated her, "After a few days, my parents will accept us. The problem is for the boy. Accepting someone else's child is not so easy. Therefore, we have to wait for somedays. Meanwhile my mother will understand it." Meanwhile, Nabin continued to withdraw money, sometimes from ATM and sometimes by cheque with the signature of Kabita. Kabita could not doubt anything. All the articles that she brought from Sudhir's house have been sold one by one, on the pretext that there is no space in the house. In simple terms, Nabin was leading a luxurious life with Kabita's money. After a few months, when the money ran out, Nabin disappeared. At first, Kabita could not know anything. But one day she went to withdraw money from the bank and found out that she had only a few hundred rupees in her bank account. The account which had lakhs of rupees a few days ago has now become empty. Now she realised that she has been squarely cheated. Saying sweet words, Nabin has looted all her possessions. What shall she do now? She could see only darkness all around her. There is a saying, "You cut your tongue by your own hand, then who is to be blamed!" She has earned everything for herself. To whom she will tell? There is no one else to stand by her. How she will maintain herself and bring up her son? Inside that dark house, tears were rolling down from her eyes. These tears are the only friend at the time of misery. Now she remembered her in-law's house. They were very good people. They loved her very much and her son would have remained pretty well there. He would have been a successful man after finishing his study. Now she ruined her own life along with her son's life. She caressed the head of her son who was sleeping next to her. At that moment she remembered Sudhir. Later she heard that Sudhir's health condition was very bad. It was kidney disease. He was on dialysis. It all happened due to her only. All those are the result of the severe blow she has given to them.

How could she escape after betraying so many good people? No matter how the time changes, there must be something like the consequences of Karma (action). Today she is completely ruined only due to her own misdeeds.

Full moon is shining outside but there is deep darkness inside her heart. What shall she do? What is her status now? What is the future of her and her son? She has to do something. She can not die in such a state of despair or let her son wander door to door for his survival. But what can she do? She is totally penny less. Her hand automatically reached her neck. Only this thin light weight chain and a pair of earrings remain. She can manage a few days by selling them. And she has to do something within those period for their future survival. Suddenly an idea struck to her mind. Her disturbed brain felt a little relaxed. Gradually her eyelids closed.

It was already eight in the morning. The soft rays of sun have fallen on Kabita through the glass window. She woke up. Now her head feels lighter. Those high waves of the sea are no more sweeping her mind. Rather her mind is floating like the calm water of a pool. She has to execute the plan that has crept in to her head. She will atone as she has done a mistake. It is written in the scriptures that if one makes a mistake and repents for it, then the gravity of the sin is diminished. She will not simply repent but will also atone. And whoever has tempted her to do these wrong things, who has taken her in a wrong path, she will take revenge on him too. This revenge will be a part of her atonement.

She had no money with her. She sold her gold chain and earrings. Then she got down to her work. But for the full implementation of her plan, Nabin's arrival is necessary. He has gone away for nearly twenty days. His mobile indicates switch off when called. Most of the time, even when it rings, he does not respond. After thinking a lot, Kabita sent a message to him. "I have talked with Pramod babu. He will take his grand son and agrees to pay ten lakh rupees instead. We will finish the deal when you will come." Kabita knows that he will come definitely for the sake of money. Exactly that happened. Nabin saw the message and replied "I came on an urgent work. Soon I will reach there. After they take custody of the child, we will fix our marriage date."

Kabita realizes that all these are lies. If Nabin will come, it is only for the purpose of money. However, the hunter is coming to be hunted. Meanwhile, Kabita also collected some information about Nabin. This is his profession. His job is to trap the daughters, daughters-in-law of good families and extort money through them, either alluring them for marriage or in some cases by blackmailing. There are several police cases against his name. He had already married in his village. A few days later his wife died. People are saying that he killed her. What she should have known before, she learnt much later. By that time, it was too late. Leave it! What is the use of thinking about all this. She was waiting for Nabin to came.

One day, after about four or five days, suddenly Nabin arrived. He started his usual talks. He showed sweet dreams to Kabita by saying enchanting words. How their marriage will take place soon. He also displayed much affection towards her son. Kabita has understood that all these are nothing but his pretence. They have decided, "tomorrow, Nabin will take her son and go to Pramod babu's house. There, he will hand over her son to him and receive the money." Kabita smiles in her mind. Tomorrow is far away. Let this night be over first.

Slowly the evening approached. At night drinking of alcohol by Nabin is a must. He has also brought his alcohol bottle with him. While opening the bottle in the house, he said, "let us celebrate our future marriage."

Kabita said, "I have bought chicken and going to prepare it. You start your drinking."

Nabin stared at her for a while and said, "what is the matter? You are very happy to day. Where as earlier you were irritated for my drinking."

Kabita said pleasantly, "Hey! You have come after so many days. Further, I am feeling very happy that this opportunity has come."

Nabin opened the bottle. After finishing almost two pegs, Kabita brought the chicken fry and said, "you eat chicken. I am preparing another peg for you."

Happily, Nabin started munching the chicken fry. Meanwhile, Kabita poured alcohol from the bottle to a glass, added some soda and put five to six sleeping tablets in to the glass. Nabin could not know anything. By the time of drinking the third peg, one takes whatever is given to him.

After two more pegs, he was totally inebriated. Alcohol mixed with sleeping tablets, he would not get up before ten o' clock tomorrow morning. The first step of her plan was successful.

Kabita looked at the watch. It is ten o' clock at night. She has to wait for two more hours. She fed her son well, dressed him in a good attire and put him to sleep. If he falls asleep now, then there is no possibility of waking up till the morning. Her chest was pounding. How everything will be done correctly. She joined her hands to God. At around 11.30 pm, she wrapped her sleeping son in a blanket and went out. Pramod babu's house is Fifteen to twenty minutes away from her house. She knew that in Pramod babu's house, everyone eats and goes to sleep by ten o' clock at night. Their main gate is locked at 10 o' clock. But usually, the small gate near it is not locked at all. She walked hurriedly. She opened the small gate slowly and slipped inside. Carefully she laid her son down on their porch and kept the piece of paper, she had written earlier, next to him. It was written on it, "I am leaving the lamp of your family with you. Please take care of him very well and forgive me." She also kept some of her son's belongings which she had brought in a bag. She rang the calling bell and walked out with quick steps. Some distance away, she waited behind a tree.

The lights of Pramod babu's house lit up. Pramod babu himself opened the door. He was startled by seeing the child suddenly. After reading the piece of paper, he happily grabbed him and entered the house. Kabita had nothing more to see. She hurriedly walked towards her house. She chose this time because the second show movie ends around twelve o' clock. People are on the road at this time. So, there is no problem for a single woman to move on the road at that time of the night. Nevertheless, the second step of her plan succeeded.

Now the final step. With high palpitations of her heart, she entered the house. Nabin was sleeping on the ground as before. She dragged him to a corner. She again read the letter, she had written before.-

I was an ordinary simple girl. By the wheel of circumstances, I also got married in a good family. But I was forced to leave the house by Nabin's false promises. He had exploited me from every angle and at last threw me away. He drained me financially, mentally, physically and socially. I have only this physical body but died since long. While all the planets, Satellites are rotating around their orbits, only I am a comet who deviated from its orbit. Once out of orbit, it is not known when I will be destroyed by someone's gravitation. Nabin is the culprit. If I wanted, I could have killed him by giving some more sleeping pills to him. But I will not let him die so easily. I want the police to arrest him. Let him be tried. He should die a slow and bitter death.

My father-in-law, mother-in-law and husband are like gods. I have harassed them by lodging false cases at the instigation of Nabin. I have also defamed them and extracted money forcefully. I repent for that. Therefore, I apologise to them and want to give them something. I have already registered my name to donate my organs. I am keeping that organ donation card here. And I sincerely request that my two eyes be given to my blind mother-in-law. My kidney should be given to my husband. I have no objection for the rest of the organs to be given to any needy persons. If my eyes will be fixed on my mother-in-law, then I can see my son with those eyes. Lastly, I beg excuse from my parents, brother, and sisters. A few drops of tears fell on the letter towards the end. After reading the letter, she folded it and wrote on it-"whoever gets this letter will hand it over to the police." She put the letter on the table and kept the organ donation card next to it. Then she placed a table in the middle of the room. She tied the nylon rope, she bought earlier, to the ceiling fan and put a noose around her neck by the other end of the nylon rope. After preparing everything she climbed on the table. She knows that organs can not be harvested after long time of death. As soon as she dies, her dead body should be taken to the hospital. And only police can do it. So, after climbing on the table, she dialed 100 in her mobile. Immediately she heard, "hello! Police control room" from that side. She told, "sir, a woman is trying to commit suicide in the house number thirty-five of lane five at Vasudev Nagar." Before hearing anything from the other end, she pushed the table hard. Her body hung in the air.

***

"The saddest thing about betrayal is that it never comes from your enemies, it comes from those you trust the most." - Anonymous

The Miser

Diwali, Festival of lights, Diwali. The Villages, cities, towns and every nook and corner of the country is illuminated with lights on this new moon day of the month of Kartik. From many ages, probably since seven thousand years, this occasion is being celebrated. On this day, Lord Rama, after killing Ravan and on completion of fourteen years of exile in forest, returned to Ayodhya with wife Sita and brother Laxman. The city of Ayodhya was full of celebrations. Every palace, every house, every cottage was lit up by the light of the earthen lamps. The citizens were overwhelmed with joy. This tradition has continued to this day. But in our Odisha, it is celebrated in a slightly different manner. On that day, we are offering Obeisance to our deceased ancestors by lighting stems of the jute plant. Ancestors who descended on earth on the day of Mahalaya in the month of Aswina, exactly a month before, are bidden farewell on the day by burning the dried jute plant and lighting the sky. At that time, we used to recite,

"Oh! Ancestors, come in darkness but go in brightness. Roll on the twenty-two steps of Lord Jagannath temple. Look us with your nectar-like eyes."

The Shradha ceremony and also the calling of the ancestors (Bada Badia Daka) at Niranjan's house of sadheigarh village was already completed. Niranjan called his son Nihar to go to the village field. There will be mass calling for the ancestors. All the people of the village will pay farewell to the ancestors of the family of the former Landlord (Jamidar) of the village after performing their shradha and bada badia daka (Calling of ancestors). They will seek their blessings. Nihar is already ten years old. He can understand a little. After the mass offering, he asked Niranjan, "father! Why are all the people of this village invoking and paying homage to the ancestors of a rich family. Usually the "Shradha" is offered to the ancestor of one's own family only".

Niranjan could know that his son is old enough to understand. So, it is natural that this thing comes to his mind. Niranjan said, "It is a very long story I will tell you after reaching home."

After reaching home, Nihar asked," Will you tell?" "Let us finish our dinner first. Then I will sit comfortably and tell. It is a lengthy one." Niranjan replied.

After the dinner, he began.

This story is the history of our village Land Lord (Jamidar) Mardaraj family. Before the original story, we have to go back a bit. About hundred years ago, Harihar Mardaraj was the Jamidar. He was very powerful. At that time there was the rule of Britishers. The kings and Jamidars had unlimited power. The British Government was happy by receiving their annual revenue. After that they did not think it necessary to bother regarding any activities of these kings and Jmidars. In these circumstances there was a theft in the village temple. Some copper utensils and the silver crown of the deity was stolen. The thief was not caught despite the best efforts. Some suspected Raghunath, the son of the temple priest. They reported it to the Jamidar Harihar. At that time Harihar Mardaraj was at the pick of his fame (defame). The subjects were trembling in fear for his tyranny. Even a pregnant cow leaves the way in fear of him. Immediately he called Raghunath. The eighteen-year-old youth Raghunath did not even flinch. He replied the Jamidar, "I am a brahmin youngster. I can beg but can not steal. You are insulting me as well as our Brahmin society by alleging theft." Saying some words like this he went away. Harihar Mardaraj trembled with rage. He could not bear to see a commoner walk away after saying such words on his face. But due to lack of evidence he did not dare to do anything in front of so many people. Whatever may be, the Britishers had a rule of law. But exactly two days later Raghunath disappeared. As if he had vanished into the void. No trace of him was found. But everyone guessed what could have happened. No one could escape after retorting on the face of Harihar Mardaraj. He must have killed him by his men and concealed his body somewhere. In this matter one should go to police. But who will go? No body has the courage. Even the family of Raghunath also. His parents cried a lot and blaming their fortune, stayed quiet. But one evening during the evening Arati, in front of some people of the village, Raghunath's priest father cried and cursed that who ever killed his son would never have a son born in his family and his family would perish in time. There will be no one in the family to pay annual Shradha(offerings) to the ancestors.

It is said that blessings or curses that come out from the deepest regions of the heart get materialized. It may be a coincidence. Since then, no son has been born in the family of the Jamidar. Only daughters. Indrani Devi was the last daughter of the family. After that, there was no one left in the family.

Nihar inquired, "Where did Indrani Devi go? What happed to her Children?"

Niranjan narrated that, since only female children

were born in the Jamidar's family, they used to retain their sons-in-law in their house after the marriage of their daughters. That means they were keeping their sons-in-law in their house for ever. Similarly, Indrani Devi was married and her husband was staying here. But unfortunately, after two years of their marriage, he died of some unknown disease. How old was she then? Only twenty or twenty one year old. After that her parents repeatedly requested her to get married once again but she refused. Apart from Lands, they had vast properties. And the only heiress of this properties was Indrani Devi. Even though she was a widow, there were many good proposals coming for her marriage at that time. But she had opposed vehemently. Ultimately, her parents passed away. Indrani Devi was the only one left at the home. She knew very well that there would be on one left in her family after her. She is the last lamp of the family. Is this the outcome of the curse of that Brahmin?

According to people, she was very miser. After the independence of the country, the Jamidari system was abolished. But she still had hundreds of acres of land and gardens. Again, hundreds of years of earnings from the estates were stored in the house, outside the house and banks. On the whole, she had no problem at all. If she wanted, she could live like a king or a Jamidar. She had enough means for that. But she was living a very normal life. She did not spend unless absolutely necessary. She was not even co-operating in any developmental work of the village. She used to send away the people who came to her for help with a very small amount of money. The villagers were going to her with great hope. But she was always disappointing them.

Once the village club boys went and requested her

for help to build a library. She donated only five hundred rupees and tried to send them away. The boys expected that they would get at least ten or twenty Thousand rupees but only five hundred in lieu of that! They did not accept that money. Instead, they came out and shouted loudly, "Miser, stingy."

Once again some gentlemen of the village approached Indrani Devi and requested her to donate her land situated outside the village. They will try to establish a high school there. Village children, especially girls used to go a great distance to attend high school.

Indrani Devi did not refuse straight away. But she said, "If I will give the piece of Land, then will the school be built? You gentlemen, first show me where to get the money to construct the school building there. After that only, I will transfer the land. Otherwise, you will take the land and use it for other purpose." With grate disappointment, they had come back.

She also used to subscribe on every village festival i.e. Dashara, Laxmipuja and other functions like other villagers. Her argument was that, "There is no Jamidari now. Like everyone, she is also a common villager. She will give as much as others give. No more, no less."

She had hundreds of acres of farm land. All the lands were given on sharing basis for cultivation. Even if there was no crop or less crop in a year, she did not spare anyone. She used to collect her share. If someone was unable to pay, he was asked to give an undertaking on a stamp paper to give the required paddy in the next year. She had no mercy or attachment for anyone. She regularly paid the salaries of her household workers and the driver on time. But except this she did not help anybody at the time of their need. She had a huge mango orchard. In the mango season, all the mangoes were plucked and sold to the trader. Otherwise, the entire orchard would be given on whole sale price. No villagers get a slice of it. This was her character. A very rough, Stingy, emotionless character. Once the club boys had said, "there is no one to give a drop of water in your mouth. Why are you so greedy? If you die, we will not shoulder your corpse."

But Indrani Devi laughed on that day. The boys were astonished. Indrani Devi asserted, "I have full faith that you all will carry me to the cremation ground and complete my cremation with full dignity." The boys laughed derisively on that day.

Days, months, years rolled on like this. The villager's anger, resentment and grievances continued to grow. Once she was ill. Meanwhile she became old. Her health had deteriorated. The doctor came from the town. He advised to take her to Cuttack hospital immediately. She had a car. No problem for it. But she refused. She said, "No need to go to the hospital. If I die, I will die on the soil of this village." The doctor administered some medicines and left. The villagers did not visit her due to intense anger. Only two days later she died.

She had no one else. Getting the news, her advocate came from the town. He went and requested the village headman to arrange for her funeral. But the Chief had denied, saying that "everyone is unhappy with her. So no one will lend his shoulder for her corpse."

The lawer insisted, "you were unhappy with her but now she is dead. No one should hold a grudge against a dead person."

But the Chief did not hear anything. At last, the lawer requested to call a village meeting. Although the chief did not agree at first, but after a lot of talking he agreed.

Immediately the village meeting was called by beating the drums.

The sudden convening of village meeting like this had surprised everyone. Has it any connection with the death of Indrani Devi? Almost all the villagers attended the meeting out of curiosity.

After everyone assembled in the meeting, the lawer repeated his request. He appealed, "what has happened has already happened. Respecting the dead soul, you should cremate the dead body."

All protested in one voice. The club guys said that they would not let it happen. Why should we cremate the dead body of a person who despite her opulence, has never contributed anything to the development of the village? You take the corpse to the town by your car and do what ever you have to do there.

The lawer looked at them. Then he told, "It is all right. Respecting your wishes, I will carry Indrani Devi's body. But I will say something else before that. Before dying, Indrani Devi has written a letter for you all. She had instructed me to read it before you. I will read it if you agree."

Everyone looked at each other in surprise. Then they said together, "ok, please read it."

The lawer opened the letter and started reading.

My dear villagers;

In your eyes, I am a very low-level human being. Never helped anyone in my life. Never participated in anyone's happiness or sorrow. I am very selfish, have not spared anyone a penny. Very miser etc. etc.

Yes, I am like that. But I was forced to be like this for a purpose. All of you may know that a few years after the Mohabharat war, there was a severe famine in Hastinapur.

It was becoming very difficult to get some grains for the people to eat. Then king Judhisthir sent Bhim to bring a thousand carts of paddy from Kuber. When Bhim went to Kuber, he saw that Kuber was picking small pieces of stones from some paddies. Bhim's mind got suspicious. He, who is picking small pieces of stones from such small quantity of paddy, will he be able to give thousand carts of grain? He returned and told Judhisthir what he had in mind. Judhisthir smiled a little and again sent him back to Kuber. This time Bhim went and apprised Kuber about his intension. Immediately, Kuber gave one thousand carts of grain to Bhim. But the story is not finished yet. While Bhim was carrying the grains, the road became muddy due to heavy rains and the carts could move no further. Bhim came and told Kuber. Kuber suggested, "first, scatter five hundred carts of grain on the road, then the carts can move. I am sending another five hundred carts of grains." Bhim stared at Kuber in surprise. The man who saves paddy by pickling pebbles from it one by one, offers five hundred cart loads of grains to be dumped on the road without any hesitation. Kuber could understand the mind of Bhim and said, "wealth is accumulated little by little and spent indiscriminately for genuine works.

That is why, I used to save penny by penny. Our Jamidar family has ruled this area for hundreds of years. Some people have been subjected to exploitation. But there has been no visible improvement in this village. So, I aimed to save so much wealth that this area can be improved a lot. Therefore, towards the end of my life, I sold all the properties outside the village and all the old gold and silver I had at home and deposited them in the bank. All the details are with the lawer. Now I am giving a little guidance regarding the utilisation of this money.

First of all, I am donating my lands to those share croppers who have been cultivating it for years. They do not have to give anything to anyone. I have also transferred some properties in the name of each of my employees. So that they can spend their rest of life comfortably.

I have a lot of love for the club boys. Many times, the boys came to me with the hope that I will give them some donation, so that they can set up a library. If you have a library, where will you keep the books? So, I am giving them a piece of my land and thirty lakh rupees for construction of library house and purchase of books.

The gentlemen of the village have also requested me several times to open a high school in the village. If I gave five or ten lakh rupees, could the school have been opened? Not at all. For that, I have made full arrangements. The school will be established on the entire vacant field of mine near the village. For the school building and expenses of the school along with the salary of teachers for the first one year, you can get money from my bank through the lawer. I have made provision for it.

Apart from this, my wish is to have a hospital in our village. The people of our village and neighbouring villages are going a long way for treatment. Many patients are dying on the way. That is why, a hospital is absolutely necessary in the village. I am donating my house i.e. Jamidar's palace for that purpose and the money is also being provided for the related expenses of the hospital. But I have some conditions for all this. There is no one left in our family. You all are the heirs of my clan.

Therefore, every year on Diwali you all will pay homage to the ancestors of our family. By doing so, your accumulated anger, discontent against our family through ages will be lessened to some extent and my soul as well as the soul of my ancestors will be able to find some peace. My respectful obeisance to you all.

Yours.

Indrani Devi, the Miser

After reading the letter, the lawer removed his glasses from his eyes and wiped his face and glasses with a handkerchief. Then he said, you will be surprised to hear that Indrani Devi had kept about fifty crore rupees in her bank account only for the development of the village. Her wish was to make a committee of four or five prominent people of the village which will try to see that the money will be properly utilised as per her direction.

Then, please let me go now. I will take her dead body to the town. Her funeral rites will be performed there.

Everybody was speechless. The environment was completely silent. Even dropping of a mustard will be heard. Tears were in everyone's eyes. Now everyone understands why Indrani Devi was behaving like that. Suddenly, one of the club boys shouted- Indrani Devi, Jindabad. Long live- Indrani Devi. Every one repeated rhythmically at a time. The secretary of the club said, "what Indrani Devi said on that day, "You all will take my dead body on your shoulders and cremate it with full honour" is the truth, the right thing.

Everyone in the village got up. The dead body had to be cremated. Indrani Devi's dead body was carried around five villages in a huge procession and was cremated in the village cremation ground with full respect.

By the time he finished saying all these things, tears came to the eyes of Niranjan. He saw tears in Nihar's eyes also. Even if he is a child still he has understood something, felt something. Wiping the tears from his eyes, Niranjan said, "Now you realise why along with offering Shradha at home on Diwali, we also perform shradha ceremony in the village field and also call the ancestors. Everyone offering shradha together and praying for the salvation of the soul of Indrani Devi as well as her ancestors.

***

"A noble purpose inspires sacrifice, stimulates innovation and encourages perseverance." - Gary Hamel

The Fallen Night Jasmine

The month of Magha is coming to an end. The incoming footsteps of spring is heard slowly, the chill in the atmosphere reduced substantially. The mango trees have bloomed everywhere. The fragrance of mango flowers has filled the air. It was the second week of February. Asima got down from the town bus and was slowly walking towards her office. There is a small market on the way from bus stand to her office. Asima noticed that many greeting cards were kept attractively in many shops. Various gift items were also displayed in an appealing manner. She remembered that after a few days valentine's day will come. For that reason, all these decorations to attract the attention of customers. Everywhere, especially among young men and women, there has been an extraordinary interest and enthusiasm. Her friends have been discussing among themselves for a long time how to buy greeting cards, how to choose gifts for their male friends. The boys must also be thinking something like this. But very few people probably know who this valentine is. Saint Valentine was actually a Christian priest who was executed and beheaded on 14th February 269 AD. He had nothing to do with this love affair. It was the medieval English poet Geoffrey Chaucer who, in the 14th Century, portrayed February 14 as a day of love in his poetry and associated it with saint valentine. Then in the modern era, the business men expanded its spread greatly with their alluring advertisements. As a result, their business is worth hundreds of crores. Even though it is not a part of our culture, our society has somehow accepted it.

Leave it. What does it have to do with her? For her, this Valentine's Day has no significance. When one is struggling to live from moment to moment, there is no mentality for an emotional thing like love. It has been five years since she has a smile on her face or a glimpse of happiness seen on the face of her parents. Now-a-days she is coming out a little bit as luckily she got a job in a private institution due to the help of an N.G.O. She reached the office. It was the same situation all the day. The same discussion was going on among the young girls of her age. How they will enjoy the valentine's day? What gifts they will purchase, in which hotel they will take their food. She felt very uncomfortable. Of course, no one was talking or discussing about it with her. Somehow the office was over. She breathed a sigh of relief and took the bus again and reached home.

Her mind was getting heavy. After taking dinner early, she went to sleep. But where is the sleep? All the past events danced in her mind.

She has already crossed twenty-five springs. Twenty-five may be wrong. Twenty springs and five hot summers. If not summer, what else? Last five years she has been living in tremendous heat wave and hot atmosphere. She is not living a normal life but living like a dying person. All her smiles and happiness have vanished somewhere due to her ill luck. She is worthless like a fallen night jasmine. Blooming in the calm and fragrant atmosphere of the night, the night Jasmie flower falls from the tree when exposed to the morning sun rays. It can have no further use. It is written in its fate that it will be crushed and eliminated under the feet of passing walkers or under the wheel of a speeding vehicle. She is now only a fallen night jasmine. She is waiting for her end by someone's strike or someone's cruelty or some one's negligence.

What was her fault for which she is suffering so much? She is the daughter of an ordinary middle-class family. She had no such big hopes and aspirations. From school to college, all her education are in this town only. Her life was going well. There was neither the joy of spring nor the mirage of the desert. Everything was so calm, simple and easy. At that time, she was a student of the second year of plus three. This trouble started from the beginning of the year. Abinash, a student of her college, fell after her. As per his reverie, he loved her very much and cannot live without her. He was trying to come closer to her by saying all these sweet words. But Asima was as stable as a slab of stone. The big waves of Abinash's love returned unsuccessfully after hitting the stone wall. She knew what the definition of love is for the boys of these days. Actual love is a selfless, all - encompassing love that expects nothing in return. A beautiful, natural, clean, pure feeling. But now love is another form of desire and deception. Further love is generated between two people due to affection and admiration for each other. But now a days, one way, two way even three-way love has become reality. Asima made up her mind. She has no business in all this. Even, she once tried to explain these things to Abinash. She said, "Look Abinash! You have come to a wrong place. I have no attraction or weakness towards you or anybody else. I do not want to enter in to these complicated matters. I have come to college for study. That is only my work. So, please stay away from me." But Abinash was not in a position to understand it. He started moving after her as before. And according to his actions, the impression on him began to change in Asima's mind. Further, she thought of ways to get rid of him.

On that day, as usual, she was going to college on a bicycle with two of her friends. On the half way, Abinash overtook them on a motorcycle. After some distance, she saw, as if he was waiting for them. Seeing them, he said to Asima, "stay a while. I have something to say." But Asima ignored and passed him on her bicycle. Abinash went behind her and pulled her scarf (dupatta). Luckily Asima escaped from falling down. Immediately she got down from the cycle and said in a rude voice, "How dare, you are pulling my dupatta." Meanwhile her two friends arrived there. Two or three friends of Abinash also reached there. Both sides started arguing with each other. Gradually people were also gathering on the spot. Suddenly Ashima's brother arrived with some of his companions. They started beating Abinash. The friends of Abinash fled from the place. No matter how strong the people doing the wrong thing, they do not have the courage to face the truth. Abinash was thrashed black and blue. His cheeks and lips were injured and blood were oozing from there. Ashima tried to stop it. But her brother and none of his friends stopped. Finally, they warmed him not to repeat this in the future and let him go. Abinash who was completely humiliated and also angry walked away after giving a hard stare to Ashima.

Asima was watching how his face was burning with extreme anger. But due to the helplessness of not being able to do something, the fire that was burning was diminished. But who knows if a light wind blows it will not ignite again. Ashima's body shivered.

On that day, after coming from the college she was thinking, this is how the Mahabharata war had happened. Duryodhana had gone to Indraprastha, invited by king

Yudhishthira, to the royal sacrifice (Rajasuya Yagna) in Dwapara Yuga. There he was looking to the palace of Indraprastha which was built by demon Maya. While he was walking around with his brothers, he saw a small pond full of water in front of him. He had to cross it. When he lifted his royal robe, he realised that it was only a floor. But it was creating an illusion of pond. After going some distance, he saw the same kind of scene. While walking on it unhesitatingly thinking it as a floor, he perceived that it was actually a swamp. He fell into the water and got completely drenched. His royal clothes became wet. Meanwhile, at some distance, Draupadi was enjoying all these in the company of her friends. Spontaneously the words "blind man's son is blind" came out of her mouth. That means, as Duryodhana's father Dhritarashtra was blind, so he is also behaving like a blind person. It was here that the seeds of Mahabharata war were sown. As a result, the entire Kauravas and Pandavs were destroyed. In the anger of that insult, Duryodhana tried to make Draupadi naked in full royal court. In the war the Kauravas were completely annihilated and the Pandavas were able to save their linage with much difficulty.

Therefore, this insult is like a wild fire. It will gradually spread and destroy everything. Can Abinash do anything like that? further she was thinking that he would not dare to look towards her due to the thrashing he got on that day. But the difference between courage and adventure is very small. She will have to tread cautiously for a few days. Now her brother is taking to and picking her from the college on a motorcycle. After a few days everything will return to normal by itself.

Actually, it was back to normal. She had almost forgotten all the matters. Abinash was also not coming near her. She was somehow relieved. But she could not realise that this is the lull before the storm. That day was fixed for the form fill-up in the college. They will almost stop coming to the college after form fill-up. So that was practically the last day in the college. All friends came together on that day. Her brother dropped her off at the college. She told her brother not to come to pick her up. Because she did not know how much time will take for the form fill-up. Further, she had confidence that she could go home in the company of her friends. On that day many friends had come together. Time passed with much funfair. Form filling was also completed on time. For some further work, she was climbing the stairs to the first floor with one of her friends. At that time Abinash was descending from the first floor. She was going up ignoring him. Just as the two were nearer, Abinash threw some liquid on her face from a bottle, he was hiding behind him and ran away. At first, Ashima did not understand anything. She felt as if some water splashed on her face. It felt cold for one or two seconds. But then it seemed as if there was a fire. She experienced as if the flesh and skin of her face began to melt away. She screamed repeatedly in unbearable pain and fainted.

By the time she regained consciousness, she found herself in the hospital. Her face, neck and hands were affected by the acid. The ointment was applied all over her face. There was severe pain in one of her eyes. She was in severe agony despite the doctors giving her pain-relieving injection. At that time, she could know that she had been attacked by acid. She shivered. The mental tension was much more than physical pain. Acid attack …! That means … what would be the condition of her face? She knew how the faces of girls become distorted after being attacked by acid. But what can she do now? Now the first priority is to save her life. Death would relieve this physical and mental pain. But she did not want to die. She wanted to punish the person who is responsible for her present condition. So, she has to live. Not only for her, but for all women who have been attacked by acid and to show Abinash the fruits of his action. The human body is built in such a way that the courage, patience come naturally to face any difficult situation. Amidst the darkness of severe pain, Ashima could visualize the light of hope. A person needs a positive mental state as much as he needs medicine to get rid of pain. One can confront any problem if he is mentally strong. He can also face any situation. She was kept in I.C.U. Outsiders were not allowed to go inside. She could see her father, mother, brother outside the glass wall of the room by her one eye only. Doctor came and injected her an injection. Perhaps a sleeping injection. Her eyelids were slowly closing.

She was undergoing treatment in a government hospital. Because the private hospitals usually turn away such patients with various excuses. Further, the amount of expenses there is very high, which is beyond the capacity of her father. The treatment was going on for nine months. Her life was saved but her face was completely disfigured. One of her eyes was fully damaged. She returned to her house after nine months and while looking at her face in the dressing table mirror for the first time, she screamed abruptly. She realised that all her future in this life was darkened. In fact, the girls who recovered from the acid attack suffer from depression, insomnia, nightmares and anticipation of further attacks, apart from the physical scars. The scope of their thinking revolves around all these matters. Ashima was also passing through the same circumstances. She was thinking that she could not find a job with such an ugly face. The question of marriage will not arise. People will look at her with pity but who will marry her? Then what is her future? Will she live like this for the rest of her life?

The worries of Brundaban Babu, Ashima's father, was increased many folds. While discharging from the hospital, the doctor advised him to treat Ashima in a good hospital. After conducting eight to ten plastic surgeries her face will become a bit normal. The eye will look a little better if the damaged eye can be replaced with an artificial eye. But these require a lot of money. Where will this money come from? Whatever property available in the village are all ancestral properties. All brothers have a share in it. They will not agree to sell them and the gold ornaments available in the house are not so much. It is, "like a conch of water compared to the sea." His head was spinning. Then the poor girl will spend her whole life like this. He cannot do anything as a father. He was writhing in the depths of despair.

When all the doors of hope closed for a man, the darkness of despair covers everywhere, at that time, somewhere a door is kept open for him by God through which a faint ray of hope shows the direction.

Akash's house is in the same colony, in the backyard of Ashima's house. The relationship between the two families is very cordial. After completion of his engineering, Akash is working in a private company. He came home after almost a year. As per his habit, he came to Ashima's house. Till then, he did not know anything about the misfortune of Ashima. No one from his house told him about this.

At first, he was shocked when he saw her. He has been watching Ashima since childhood. What has happened to a clam, simple, sweet and beautiful girl? He was totally disturbed. The whole family has been pushed to the deep depths of uncertainty due to the incident like this. Not only Ashima alone, but the entire family is suffering for her. There is no smile on anyone's face. Sometimes a person reaches such a stage of time where only the call of his heart echoes in his ears, and he becomes determined to do a particular work consciously or unconsciously. That had happened with Akash. At that place and at that moment, he spontaneously took a decision to provide Ashima better treatment and try to restore her face as before, to some extent as far as possible.

Now-a-days, you can know everything by searching the internet. Akash was able to locate a hospital in Hyderabad, his place of working, where such patients are successfully undergoing plastic surgery. He sent all the old medical papers of Ashima to the doctor there by e-mail.

The doctor informed that the treatment will continue at least for two years. Eight to ten plastic surgeries have to be conducted and each surgery will cost around two lakh rupees.

Akash is a guy not to be defeated easily. He has contacted some N.G.O.s at Hyderabad and requested them for financial assistance. Further he appealed financial help on social media in the name of Ashima and her father. That is called crowd funding. In this a lot of people pay a few bucks which ultimately helps to pay for the whole treatment over the time. The stream of financial help came to the bank account of Ashima's father. There are still some kind people among us who help, as per their capacity, others in their difficult times. After having sufficient funds, he planned to admit Ashima in the hospital. Her mother will accompany her. His place of work is at Hyderabad. So, it will be convenient for him also. An NGO has agreed to look after her for the rest of works.

On an auspicious day, they had started their journey. Sitting on the train, Ashima was thinking, can she really get rid of the black glasses and the scarf covering her whole face? Can she really go out with her uncovered face? will she actually be freed? She was remembering the story of Ahalya. Ahalya of Treta Yuga. Her husband, Saint Gautam, had cursed her to turn into a stone due to her mistake, knowingly or unknowingly. She was lying like that as a slab of stone in the deep forest. The condition was, if Lord Rama's foot ever touches that rock, Ahalya will regain her original form. After abduction of Sita, while Rama Chandra was passing though that forest, the stone Ahalya was transformed into feminine Ahalya by the touch of his feet. Ahalya was reborn. Like that Ashima also turned into a stone. Can Ramachandra in human form will come to her, at whose touch she will rise again with full blossom and joy? Tears fell from her good eye. She knew that it was just a mirage, far from reality.

Asima was admitted in the hospital at appropriate time. A few days later she had her first plastic surgery. Actually, plastic surgery is a two to four hours job. But she was discharged from the hospital only after three days. Again, the second surgery will be after two to three months. Akash had arranged a small house in Hyderabad for them to stay near the hospital. However, with the help of Akash, her treatment was successfully completed and her face, though not as beautiful as before, did not look so disfigured. Again, an artificial eye was implanted in the place of the eye that was completely damaged. Overall, the ugliness of the face was reduced to some extent. They came back to their hometown. And now Ashima is working in that private company with the help of an NGO. The doctor has assured her that if anyone ever donates an eye, then her eye can be restored.

X X X X X X

Abinash was spending his days in jail. All his activities were proved from the CCTV footage of the college. Many college students also testified against him. The case was decided early and he was sentenced to ten years rigorous imprisonment under section 329 E of the Indian penal code. But Ashima was not satisfied with this. This punishment is nothing for a person who destroyed the sweet dream of a girl, degraded her mentally, physically and financially and left her to suffer for the rest of her life. After ten years he will come back and lead a normal life. Therefore, Ashima told her lawyer to file an appeal in the higher court. So that he would be sentenced to life imprisonment. He can no longer move in the civilised society or cause such a disaster to anyone. For this cause, many organisations in Odisha are helping her. It has transformed into a mass movement. Ashima fell asleep amidst all these thoughts.

She was awakened by the alarm of her mobile. It is already six in the morning. She has to get ready and go to office. She does not feel like going to the office today. Because today is 14th February, valentine's day. All the staffs of the office, whether they are youth or old, are looking forward to enjoy it. Various plans are being made. But she is an exception. What taste remains in a burnt curry. Whose path is thorny, what tenderness this valentine's day bouquet can offer? She feels very sad that people comment on her even though she has done nothing wrong. It is even more sorrowful that the girls are commenting more than the boys. Even she had applied for leave today. But the manager forced her to come. She reached her office. There was almost no work today. Everyone was in pleasant mood. The manager came and announced, "this evening there is a party in a hotel. All employees must join the party. They can also bring their spouses or partners."

Ashima did not really want to join the party. But the manager himself requested her and even arranged the office vehicle for her to come and go. How could she not have come?

The party started on time. Two persons at every table. Whether married or unmarried, everyone was enjoying the festivities with their companions. But Ashima was sitting alone. She had no partner. She was feeling very awkward. She was not at all interested in this colourful event. Will not the feeling of inferiority complex arouse in her mind after seeing the merry making and celebrations of other people?

Suddenly, manager babu said loudly, "welcome, welcome." Ashima looked that side and saw that Akash is entering the party hall. How is he here? Her surprise knew no bounds. Akash came straight to her and sat on the chair. Before Ashima could understand anything or say anything, he said, "There is nothing to be surprised about. Manager babu is my old acquaintance. The purpose of my coming here is that I Have some important talks with you."

What will Akash say? She had already seen him, knew him even though she had not interacted or talked much with him. As he tried very hard to restore her disfigured face and ultimately succeeded in it, her head bowed down at the thought of it. There may exist such kind of people in this world. It must be. Otherwise, how could this earth survive? She looked at Akash's face.

With much reluctance, Akash said, "the matter is, I love you, want to marry you. Do you agree." Her whole body trembled with the tremor of excitement. The glass of cold drink in her hand shook a little. As he was extremely busy for her treatment, some kind of attraction had flashed in her heart for a moment. Immediately she restrained herself from it. She even scolded herself for her adventurous attitude. But, what is she listening today?

There will be no shortage of girls for a handsome man with such a strong personality. But he wants her. Can a flower that has fallen in a storm be offered to God? Has she a great luck like this?

Hey! Why are you thinking so much? I need an answer. Ashima became normal in the words of Akash. She said, "but...."

Without letting her say anything, Akash said, "I already knew you. Believe me, I did not have any weakness. But now, after you returned from Hyderabad, I felt that you have occupied a place in my heart. That's why I spoke to your manager and waited for today. The beauty of a person is temporary. It fades over time. That is why, it is said, "Beauty is skin deep". You are pure and holy. Why do you feel inferior for someone's cruelty?

Ashima could not say anything else. She lowered her face.

"Silence is the sign of consent." Akash could understand it. He handed over her the rose flower, he was hiding. Immediately the place was resonated with the applause of the employees present there. As if somebody had sprinkled red powder on the face of Ashima. While stretching her hand with embarrassment, she wondered how the world had suddenly changed for her. The party she did not want to attend, now looks as colourful as the seven colours of a rainbow. The sweet sound of music enchanted her. All foods and drinks tested like nectar. Actually, one never knows when what time will come in one's life. This earth changes its colour every moment. She had observed humanity in Akash, but now she could know that he is as clear and great as the sky, that his heart is so vast and expansive.

After the party, Aksh offered to drop her home in his car. Ashima did not object. While sitting in the car, she remembered an incident happened a long time ago. One morning, while standing on the balcony, she was surprised to see a gentleman picking the flowers that had just fallen from the night - Jasmine tree in front of her house and placed them in a polythene bag. She asked him, "how will these fallen flowers be offered to god?"

The gentlemen replied, "the night Jasmine flowers bloom at night and fall in the morning. However, the freshly fallen flowers can be used in the worship of God. It just depends on the mentality of the person who offers it."

In fact, the words of that day became a reality in her life today. Like a fallen night Jasmine, she too can be used for the worship of God. A change is also possible in the fortunes of fallen night jasmine.

***

"I saw that you were perfect, and so I loved you. Then I saw that you were not perfect and I loved you even more." - Angelita Lim

The Unexpected

It is a small village. Name is Bijan Pur. A small river is passing by it with gurgling sound. The ambience of the village, full of trees and vines, is very clam, beautiful and sweet. Since time immemorial, the village has passed through the foot print of time very smoothly. There is no obstacle, no enmity or dispute. An atmosphere full of love and affection. Today, however, the calm atmosphere has been eclipsed. An incident happened in the village that had been uneventful for years. That event is the main topic of today's discussion.

The news that was telecasted on TV in the morning has left everyone stunned. The children, Oldmen and youths of the village are all gathered in the porch of the house of Das babu. Everyone is worried. The people are passing different kind of remarks. All the channels are reporting that incident, the description of the tragic occurrence- "During heavy rain last night while continuing its journey, the Chennai- Puri express train met with an accident on a bridge near Rajahmundry in Andhra Pradesh. As a result, some compartments of the train have fallen in to the river. Many people have died and injured. Some are not found. The rescue operation is going on extensively."

His body is shivering in unknow fear. The mind is becoming restless. Tears are falling from eyes of Anil. He is praying God in his mind, "may everything be fine." About twenty days ago, he had sent his parents on pilgrimage of four holy places (chari Dham). First, they (Das Parents) went to Delhi in purusottam express. From there they had gone to Badrinath, then Dwarika and finally they visited Rameswar and was returning to Puri via Chennai. They would return to the village after visiting Lord Jagannath at Puri. Their train tickets in the three tier air-conditioned coach were reserved earlier. Their coach number was B-3 in the Chennai-Puri express. But what happened? Accident! According to the reports all the air-conditioned coaches have fallen in to the river. What has happened to father & mother? All three sons are crying continuously. All the people gathered there are praying. Some have gone to the Vishnu temple, Goddess temple to lit the lamps. Everyone's prayer is, "Somehow the Das couple should escape from the accident and return back in good health."

This is the speciality of the village, the sweet smell of the village. When someone is suffering, the supportive and sympathetic hands of others reach him. Everyone is equally saddened by one's suffering.

The father of the Das family is Dibakar Das. He was a successful farmer of his time. He used to grow two crops annually on his ancestral land and maintained his family. His family consists of three sons and a daughter. After the birth of his eldest son Anil, there was no more child born for many years. His wife wanted a daughter. Eight years after Anil's birth, she become pregnant after a lot of worship to gods and goddesses. A son was born. Later another son. Finally, a girl came to her lap. Dibakar provided education to Anil with much difficulties. He also studied well. As there was no high school in the village, he kept Anil in a hostel in a distant town for his study. Anil continued his study in the college after high school. After graduation Anil took B.Ed. training and became a teacher in a high school in the nearby town. After getting the job he helped his father and shouldered all the responsibilities of the family. He accorded education to his younger brothers and sister who were much younger than him. He also got his sister married He had to work hard for this. He tutored some children in the morning and evening to earn some extra money. Being a math teacher, he was in demand for tuition. Despite all this, he bought a large plot of land in the outskirt of the village. Again, since the house of the forefathers was small, he also built a house on that land, so that everyone could stay there. Of course, for that he availed a loan from the bank and paid it in due time. Now all are staying in that house. His younger brothers did no study well. So, they could not get any job but doing small businesses for their livelihood. They are already married. Dibakar is no longer able to cultivate. The lands have been given on sharing basis. Anyway, the family life was rolling smoothly. Suddenly, this untimely thunderbolt has stunned everyone.

The Odisha Government has announced that the next of kin of those who were traveling in that ill-fated train will be taken to the accident site free of charge. By doing so, they can identify the bodies of their dead relatives or attend the injured ones. All kinds of financial assistance will be provided to them.

Now the question is who will go to the accident site. Anil's condition is bad. About eight days ago one of his legs was fractured in a motor cycle accident. That leg is plastered. After fifteen days the plaster will be opened. So, he asked both the younger brother to go. He also gave some money to them. Two brothers, Ajit and Asit, went to the temple early in the morning and visit the God, took flower of the mother Goddess, and left for the site. They have to go to Jatani and from there by rail to the place of accident.

By the time they reached the accident site, it was already fourth day of the disaster. The scene there was heart-wrenching. Heaps of dead bodies were put in a temporary house and covered with white sheets. The relatives are going around identifying the bodies of their kith and kin. Weeping and crying created a melancholic atmosphere in the area. Ajit and Asit first started towards the hospital where the injured were being treated. A man lives with hope. They also had a hope that possibly their parents were only injured and being treated and they would have escaped death. Due to the lack of space in the hospital, two temporary hospitals were erected. They searched the list of patients in each hospital. Neither the name of father Dibakar Das nor his wife Kamini Devi were in the lists. Stil hopeful, they verified each bed in all hospitals with bated breath. But no…not found anywhere. Then the turn to look at the dead bodies. The corpses were lined up. No matter how much ice, chemicals were applied, the corpses had started smelling.

Two brothers covering their noses with handkerchiefs started searching the dead bodies. The corpses were very bloated as they were recovered from the river. It had been four days. It was hard to figure out. No body was recognisable. All seemed the same.

They stopped next to the two bodies lying together. They took off the cloak and observed that they were of a man's and women's. Although they were not identifiable, seeing the bag and small vanity bag near their heads, they could know that both of them were their father and mother. Eagerly, they looked inside the bags. A photo of their family was found along with some money. Then they were completely sure that those two dead bodies were their father and mother. After informing the local authorities and completion of all formalities, the cremation of the bodies were done by the help of a local volunteer organisation. The incineration of two bodies was held on a single pyre.

They had informed this tragic news to their home by telephone. After the cremation and collection of bones, ashes, they returned and reached home after two days. The entire village was mourning by crying and shrieking. Anil's grief was inexpressible. It was such a situation that he could not even see the dead face of his parents. Amidst the tears and sorrowfulness, the funeral rites were completed. All the rituals like the tenth day bathing in the pond, the Shradha on the twelfth day, village feast and then the sankirtan were performed as per the prescribed method. The end of a generation had taken place.

An end creates another beginning. The trouble started at home after less than a month of Dibakar's death. Their love and affection for each other had vanished. It was Ajit and Asit who started all the problems. They wanted separation which means division of paternal properties. Even they wanted a share from the house, Anil had built. Their eyes were also on that land. One engineering college has come up near it. As a result, shops, market have also been cropped up. Therefore, the price of land has increased substantially. Anil bought about half an acre of land as it was available at a low price. But he purchased it in the name of his father, Dibakar. Usually, this happens in a middle-class family. Until the father is alive, all the lands that are bought is in his (father's) name. Because he is the guardian of the house. But now, the brothers want a share, assuming it as their father's property. Sister, Iti, has also joined them. She too wants a share. Brothers and sister, even many people in the village know that no one has any contribution for it. Still, they are insisting to get their share. When a man is engrossed by lust, he does not hesitate to break the cord of relationship. Observing this kind of attitude of his brothers and sister, Anil felt a lot of pain. He has no greed for anything. But he has two daughters, their education and marriage. He planned that he would sell a portion of the land and get his daughters married. Now what will happen? He remembered that once his father told him in the course of discussion, "You have worked so hard to acquire this house and land. I will not deprive you from your rights." He knew that his father had made a will and gave it to the village Sarpanch. He had also gone to the Sarpanch. But Sarpanch Bhabani Pradhan denied. He said, "he has not given me any will. Perhaps he has not prepared it."

After retuning disappointed from there, Anil called his brothers and said, "I have spent all my earnings of my life for you. I have acquired all this house and land. Then why this partition? We will live together as before. There is no problem."

But they were not in a position to listen. This is how the world has become these days. Man does not look at anything expect his own interest. He does not hesitate to sacrifice his father, mother, brothers and sisters for his own benefits. Ajit said directly, "We do not mind what you have done earlier. Father should have done his duty towards us. You did because he could not. You helped our father not us. Now as per the law, the properties of the father will be divided. We have already called a village meeting. The meeting will be held after two days. There, the decision will be taken as to who will take which part."

Anil was surprised. Indeed, this age has changed so much. While purchasing the land, wife Basundhara advised, "You are paying all the money. You should buy the land in your name. Then there will be no problem in the future." But he did not listen. Rather he was angry with her. He has never considered himself separate from his family i.e. his father, mother, brothers, and sister. For that, he purchased the land in the name of his father, the guardian of the family. While constructing the building, he made two rooms for his two brothers, one room for parents, two rooms for himself and one room for his sister for the convenience of all. Everyone was also very happy. But soon after the death of parents, the partition issue started. Basundhara is sitting with a sullen face. Time and again she was telling him sarcastically, "Have you seen? You have taken so much care of your brothers. What happened now? The persons whom you have raised and established in the society have deceived you."

Anil could not speak anything. Only he uttered this much, "keep faith on God."

Two days later the village meeting was held. Surprisingly, Starting from Sarpanch Bhabani Pradhan to all other gentlemen, opined that "father's property will be divided in to four parts." Anil was compelled to open his mouth. Politely he said, "I have acquired all these land and house myself. At least some more parts should be given to me. I have the responsibilities of my two daughters. My retirement time is also approaching. If this land will be divided in to four parts, then what will remain for me?" Some people supported him and said, "He is the elder brother. So, he has the right to get some more portions." But all the main people spoke for four parts. Much time elapsed in such arguments. Nothing could be decided. It was decided that the meeting would be held once again after five days and a decision would be taken.

It was 6 P.M on that day. The meeting will begin shortly. But before a day the electric connection was completely cut off due to a severe storm. There was darkness all around. Once electricity goes off in the village, it is not known when it will come back. Ajit and Asit were desperately trying to arrange petromax lights. They had captured the sarpanch and two other main persons of the village, so that the decision will go in their favour. Meanwhile, they had claimed compensation from the railway authorities. They will get sixteen lakh rupees as compensation i.e. eight lakh rupees each for father and mother. This too will be shared among all.

Anil was sitting quietly. He would accept whatever happens. What else can he do when his own blood has betrayed him? The meeting started on time. The meeting venue way brightly illuminated by four petromax lights. The minds of Ajit and Asit were dancing with joy. Land with compensation money. They were conceiving many plans in their minds. As if by dying, their father and mother filled their pockets. After sometime of discussion and arguments, the sarpanch was prepared to pronounce his decision. All eyes and ears were fixed on him. As the sarpanch cleared his throat to declare his decision, a bright ray of light from the entrance of the village caught everybody's attention. That moving ray of light was coming towards the meeting venue at high speed. That was the auto rikshaw of Binay of that village. The auto came straight to the meeting place and out of it came an Oldman and an old woman. Their faces were clearly visible in the bright petromax light. Everyone was stunned. Had they seen ghosts? They were the dead Dibakar Das and his wife.

Dibakar went straight and stood in the middle of the meeting place and said in a loud voice, "this Dibakar Das is alive till now. So, there is no need to divide the house. And everyone Listen, only Anil has the right to this property. Because of his high-mindedness, he bought everything in my name. No brother or sister has a right in it. I had made a will and given it to sarpanch Bhabani Pradhan. Then why this meeting now?" By that time Bhabani Pradhan had already fled. Looking at Ajit and Asit who were standing there, Dibakar said, "of course, I gave half of the land in the will to my two younger sons. But now nothing will be given. The ungrateful ones." Burning with anger, Dibakar Stepped towards the house. Kamini Devi, Anil and some villagers followed.

As if the sky had fallen on the heads of Ajit and Asit. All the imaginations, speculations were vanished. They could not think of anything. They had cremated the bodies. Then how about this unexpected arrival of their father and mother? In that case, whose bodies had they burned. Many questions arose in their minds.

After reaching home, Anil embraced his father and mother and started crying. Emotionally he said, "I did not believe that anything bad could happen to you. God saved us. There is a saying-no one can kill if God saves you."

Everyone was staring in wonder. How could the dead men become alive again? Realising the mood of the gathering people, Anil said, please wait a moment. Let my parents take bath and have a cup of tea, then they will tell about the incident."

Wife Basundhara paid obeisance to her in-laws, went to the kitchen for making tea. Ajit and Asit were standing with gloomy faces.

After taking tea, Dibakar narrated-on the way back to Puri by train, at around 10 PM, the train was passing on a lengthy bridge. The people say that if anyone throws some coins to the river and prays for something then his prayer will be fulfilled. Both of us got up from our seats and stood near the gate of the train compartment and threw coins in to the river. While getting up from our seats, we handed over our hand bags to the couple sitting in front of us. The accident happened when we were tossing the coins. Our compartment shook vigorously with a Loud sound. Before we could think of anything, the coach was detached from the train and fell in to the river. After that we did not know anything.

After regaining consciousness, I discovered myself in a low thatched house. At first nothing was remembered but gradually I remembered everything. The servicing and nursing of those tribals healed us completely. The fact was that when the accident occurred, we both embraced each other in panic. Since we were near the gate, we must have hurled forward and fell in to the river. We were swept a long way by the strong current of the river. We had floated about sixty to seventy kilo meters away from the crash site and were stuck on the shore in a heavily populated tribal area. The tribals of that village rescued us. The area is so remote that the nearest hospital is far away. No government employee visits that place. So, they treated us in their own way. It took us around fifteen to twenty days to recover. Even if we remembered everything, we could not send any message. The headman of the village sent a man to the block office to inform about us. Actually, that had worked. Knowing that some strangers had come to the tribal area, the local BDO came immediately in his Jeep. After hearing everything, he took us from that place and put us on a train from a nearby station with financial help. I could not remember anyone's phone number. So, no message could be sent. It was a blessing in disguise. Otherwise, the true character of our children would not have been known. I feel ashamed to see this kind of attitude of my children who were brought up with good education and culture. While the innocent tribals have helped and shown so much sympathy to the strangers, here the brothers are trying dishonestly to cheat their own brother. This is the difference between simple tribals and our civilised educated people.

Anyway, we came and got off at Jatani station. There we were looking for an auto to come home. We met Binoy there. He came to the station to drop someone. On seeing, he embraced us. We got all the informations from him and came in his auto and reached here on time.

Someone asked a question, "Then whose bodies were cremated? How did your bags reach there?"

Dibakar explained, "As far as possible the bodies must be of that couple whom we had given our bags at the time of going to the gate. They could not get out of the coach. Our bags must have been recovered near their dead bodies."

The people returned to their respective homes. Putting his hands on the shoulders of the brothers who were sitting with sulky faces, Anil said, "why are you both sitting so dejected? Today is a happy day. Our parents have returned safely. Leave this partition talk. We will live together as before."

Immediately Dibakar remarked, "Look! How big is your brother's heart" The faces of two brothers were downcast.

Basundhara came and called them for dinner. Her mind was dazzling with happiness. When something unexpected is found, joy can not be expressed in words. It is a unique experience. Indeed, God's Mercey is immense. How did he set right everything. It is unexpected that father-in-law and mother-in-law survived such a dangerous train accident. It is also equally unexpected that they had reached the village meeting on time and saved them from this division of property. Automatically her head was bowing before that super being.

***

"The only real things in life is the unexpected things. Everything else is just an illusion." - Watkin Tudor Jones

The Aroma Of The Lies

The morning has set in. The sun is rising by spreading red colour in the eastern sky. The birds have flown away in search of food by making chirping sounds. Sabita got up quickly. She also has to arrange foods for herself and for her seven-year-old son. Whatever money was there, she bought a bread and both mother and son ate it last night. She kept two pieces of it to give her son in the morning. There is nothing for her. There is not a penny with her nor a single grain in the house. What will she do? She was out of her wit.

Sabita is a girl from a remote village. She did not read much. She dropped out from class three. Her father was a farmer. Sometimes he also worked as a daily Labourer in other houses. Shankar of the nearby village was a carpenter. He used to come to her village to do wood works. He was coming to their house as well. Over the time Shankar and Sabita developed a romantic relationship. Ultimately they ran away from their houses. Shankar took a small tin house in this slum on rent and they started their marital life. Shankar was a good carpenter. Therefore, he was able to get plenty of works. They had no problem in maintaining their family. A year later, the son Kishor was born. They were very happy. Everything was going well. But suddenly one day Shankar disappeared. He went to work in the morning and never came back. She was very much worried. What happened to Shankar? Is he okay? She prayed to God for Shankar to come back well. But she observed that he had taken all his clothes. That means… Did he leave her and ran away? Can it happen? Can one forget the relationship of so many days and attraction of his own son?

Sabita could not believe it. She was thinking that Shankar would return definitely. She waited for him with hope in her heart. Days passed but Shankar did not return. Her hope remained as a hope.

Many people said many things. One said, he saw him going to Hyderabad in the Konark Express. Another said, he fled to Kolkata. And some said, he had a relationship with another girl. Shankar had run away with her. No matter where he goes, there will be no change in Sabita's position. For her it is true that Shankar has run away. He will not come back. Now she will walk alone on the road of her life. Some arrangements have to be done to run her family. She has no guts to go back home. As she had run away from home, her father told that his daughter had died for him.

Many women and girls of that slum are working in the homes of the surrounding colonies. Some clean the dishes, some others clean the houses and some doing the cooking job. She could arrange some works for her by requesting those women. Anyway, she and her son are getting two square meals every day. She was not qualified to do anything other than this job. Even so, she started dreaming. Her son will go to school and will study a lot. For that she was ready to labour hard.

Are the wishes of the people always fulfilled? Everything happens according to God's will. That's why it is said that "God is like a rope and man is a cow, where he pulls there he goes." None can tell when and how the misfortune of a man will arrive. An incident happened in her life which made her inferior to everyone and stopped all the ways of earning. That day she returned home after work. Around two O' clock, suddenly the police arrived. Before realising anything, they searched all over the house. They found nothing but took her to the police station. It was there, she came to know that the diamond ring of Mishra babu's daughter-in-law, where she was working, had been stolen. The daughter-in-law kept the ring on the dressing table. They have written to the police that their suspicion is on Sabita who is working in their house. Nothing was found in her house. After keeping two or three hours in the police station, the police released her. But its after-effects were very severe. Mishra babu fired her. The news of this incident spread everywhere. In the result, others eventually fired her. She tried to explain vehemently that she was totally innocent and she had nothing to do with it. But no one listened to her. She became a thief without stealing. She became infamous without doing any obnoxious work. She could not find work anywhere. Later she heard that the ring was found. The daughter-in-law put the ring in the dressing table drawer, which was hidden in a heap of papers. One day it was detected while cleaning the drawer. However, Mishra babu did not reveal this out of shame and fear. He got his ring back but who will compensate for the loss sustained by Sabita?

If there is no work or no money, the hunger of the stomach will not subside. Food is required to quench the fire of belly. Everything that was in the house, even the utensils, have already been sold. Now there is nothing left with her. Void, void, absolute void. What will she do? Will she jump from the bridge to the river with her son? But she restrained herself seeing the innocent face of her sleeping son. What is the fault of this quiet, simple, naïve boy? The only fault is that he is born from her womb. No… No… No matter what happens, she will live and raise her son.

It was already eight O' clock in the morning. She woke up her son. After washing his face and hands, she gave him those two pieces of bread to eat. Kishor ate it and drank some water. Sabita also drank a glass of water. Her stomach was tormented due to hunger. There was nothing to put something in her mouth. She was angry with Mishra babu. She is in this situation because of him. Will she go and sit in protest in front of his house? What would be the benefit? He would call the police station and the police would come and forcibly throw her out. No one will realise her hunger. Even none will give a piece of stale bread.

What she will do now? Will she beg? What is the harm? A hungry person can do anything to satiate his hunger. Yes… she will beg. But the government has now declared begging illegal. There are police in the intersections. So there will be no chance of begging. Despondently, she sat down under the shade of a tree, some distance from the road junction. Her hunger grew stronger. But what else can she do except praying God. Perhaps, God must have heard her prayer. There was red signal in the nearby intersection. All the vehicles were waiting for the green light. At that time, a car stopped at a little distance from her. Perhaps, for the shades of the trees and the red signal in the traffic, the motorist parked her car there. Sabita observed that a woman was sitting on the driver's seat of the car. No one else was in the car.

Immediately Sabita told Kishor to go to the car and ask the woman some money. Kishor went to the car promptly and told the lady in a sorrowful face that "he had not eaten anything for the last two days. If she will give a few rupees then he can eat something."

The lady must be kind hearted. She got out of the car and asked Kishor about him.

Like an expert since birth, Kishor told the lady, how his father abandoned them, his mother is very sick, there is nothing to eat at home etc., etc.

Despite being given the green signal at the traffic post, the lady was talking with Kishor without showing any urgency. Finally she gave him a ten rupee note and came to the back of the car, opened the dicky and gave some biscuits and fruits from there. This was a golden opportunity for Sabita. As the lady was opening the dicky, Sabita approached the car with lightning speed, and saw a large bag on the front seat and the Lady's vanity bag behind it. As the glass window of the car was open, she reached inside, picked up the vanity bag and proceeded as usual. She had hidden the vanity bag inside her saree. The incident happened so quickly that the lady was not able to know anything. She gave biscuits and fruits in the hands of Kishor, came straight, started the car and left.

The car speeded to the left side of the front intersection and as it disappeared from the sight, Sabita turned and walked back. She saw Kishor coming from some distance. Seeing the biscuits and fruits in his hands her appetite grew even more. They went some distance and ate a few biscuits. Then they walked towards their home.

Sabita's whole body was shaking till then. She stole for the first time in her life. Did she ever think that one day she would steal. But man is a slave of circumstances. In fact, no one knows in advance what situations will arise and what he will do. Both of them rushed into their house.

Sabita was very much eager to know the contents of the vanity bag. After entering the house, she took out the bag from inside of her saree. Kishor did not know till then that she had picked up the bag. After knowing now, he said, "mother! What did you do? Why did you bring her bag? How good she was. She gave so many things to eat and also gave me ten rupees. Let us return her bag."

Sabita had already opened the bag and what she saw in it, her eyes were widened. A bundle of notes, a thick gold chain and some papers were inside the bag.

Kishor repeated his words, "Let us return her bag."

Stop it. Sabita put her hand on his mouth and said "no need to return." Do we know her? Where and to whom will we return the bag? Yes, we can deposit it at the police station. But what will we do if the police misappropriates the money and gold and blame us for it and put us in jail for theft? There is nobody to help the poor. We will lose this gold and money and be punished for being a thief. So when goddess Laxmi has come to our home, why should we neglect her? We can manage two to three months with this much of money. By then everything will be normal. May be I will be able to get some work by that time. Kishor's child mind did not understand anything. He put his hand in his pocket. While giving him ten rupees, the lady handed him a small piece of paper and said, "If needed, come to me at the address written on it. He carefully put the piece of paper back in his pocket."

Sabita once again examined the bag thoroughly. In case there is anything else. No…. Nothing else. Only those money, gold and some papers. She took out all the papers and set those on fire. The bag was also cut into small pieces by a kitchen knife and thrown in to the drain, so that it would flow away in the drain water. She hid the money and gold in different places in the house. She took some money out of it and bought pulses, rice, vegetables etc. After a long time, mother and son will eat to their heart's content. Infact, the degree of happiness and Luxury are different for each person. For a poor persons, eating hot rice and dal may be a moment of happiness or it may be a Luxury for him. But for a rich person, buying an expensive car or putting the roof on a two story or three story building can be a moment of happiness. Then can the society not give small moments of such happiness to the poor? So why are there people like Kishor, like Sabita in our society today? They have to labour hard for two square meals a day. Then what is the value of this public welfare nation? What is the need for these countless social institutions? And what is the reason for the inactivity of these government establishments?

Meanwhile three months have passed. Mother and son are maintaining their life with that money. But all your money, how big it may be, will be finished if you will sit idly and spend it. How long can they run like this. The amount of money has become less and less. Despite Sabita's best efforts, she is not getting any job anywhere. Stains on the clothes can be washed with soap. But once a person's character is stained, there is no soap to wash it away. Like that the "thief" stain on Sabita could not be erased. Whenever she went in search of work, she had to listen some adverse remarks on her. No one was ready to listen to her, no matter how much she clarified her stand. Her mind was revolting. Even though she was innocent, she became guilty. What will she do? There is no other way but to accept the fate. Only praying God to help her.

Again one month passed. All the moneys were consumed. What will she do now? She was forced to take out the gold chain. They will manage a few days by the proceeds of selling the chain. By flow of time, the time gradually changes. They will see later what to do. But if she will sell it in the nearby market, someone may doubt her.

Some people may know her also. Therefore, she went to a distant jewellery shop along with her son.

The shop was just a normal shop. Sabita asked the man who looked like the owner to sell the gold chain. As the man wanted to see the chain, Sabita removed the chain from inside her saree and showed it to him. The shop keeper took a good look at the chain and asked her where from she got the chain.

Sabita was already prepared for such a question. So, immediately she said," What do you mean by 'got it'. My father gave it to me at the time of my marriage. She has come to sell it because her husband has left her and she is short of money."

The shop keeper looked at her, then said, "It is fine. This is a big chain having good gold. It will be over one lakh rupees. Do you accept cheque or cash?"

Sabita said, "Sir, we are not accustomed to Bank. We are hand to mouth people. I need cash."

The shop keeper said, "Ok. You sit here. We do not have that much of money. I am sending a man to get money from the bank."

Mother and son sat on the nearby sofa. A man brought water and tea on a tray. While sipping tea, Sabita was thinking "how much would be a lakh of rupees? It must be too much anyway. She never heard that word." She started floating in a dream of happiness.

As if wandering in the kingdom of dream, she suddenly crashed and fell on the ground. A police officer was standing in front of her and asking, "where did you get this chain?"

The fact was that, the shop keeper was suspicious after seeing such a valuable chain. Is not this a stolen gold chain? Because he knew that, buying stolen gold is also a crime. Again the appearance of Sabita was not suited at all to such an expensive gold chain. So he made her sit down and called the police.

Sabita could understand that all these were the tricks of the shop keeper. Her mouth was getting dry. However, without fear, she answered the same thing, "my marriage time chain."

The police were not satisfied with this answer. They took the mother and son to the police station. There also they asked many questions to her. But Sabita had the same answer.

Finally, finding no other option, the police took Sabita to her home. After seeing the condition of the house their suspicion was strengthened. It was a one-room tin house. After a thorough search of the house, nothing was found. Only a visiting card was found by the police. Which was given by that lady to Kishor on that day. Kishor kept it with great care.

The police officer took a good look at the card. That card belonged to the eminent social activist Mrs. Sabitri Palatasing. The police again brought the mother and son to the police station. The police officer, like twiddling a stick in the dark, called in the whatsApp number on the visiting card and also sent a photo of the chain, asking her whether the chain belongs to her or not.

After receiving a reply in affirmative, the police requested her to come to the police station.

Soon Sabitri Devi reached the police station. Totally unaware of all these events, Sabita suddenly saw Sabitri Devi in the police station and was shocked and frightened. By seeing Kishor, Sabitri Devi also remembered the incidents of that day and had an idea of what had happened.

Sabita was thinking, without stealing, the slur of theft

was already attached to her. Now she will become a real thief and go to jail. Then what will happen to Kishor? Her body was shivering. Meanwhile, the police took Sabitri Devi to them and said, "she is the thief of your chain. Please write a complaint to us. We will return your chain and put her in the lockup.

Sabita was sweating. She tried to speak something but no wards came out of her mouth. Kishor also trembled in fear out of an unknown danger.

But Sabitri Devi was completely calm. She looked at the mother and son once. Then she told the police, "who told you that this woman stole the gold chain? A few days ago I gifted her this chain."

Sabita was surprised to hear this. Even the police could not accept this easily. He asked again, "Madam ! Are you saying the correct thing?"

Yes, yes. I remember perfectly. Do not worry at all. Please return the chain to her and let us go.

After hearing this from Sabitri Devi, the police officer had nothing to say. He returned the chain to Sabita and let them go. Sabitri Devi took them out and asked them to sit in her car to go to her house.

Sabita could not believe what had happened. Obeying her, she sat in the car but her body was shaking with fear. Why is she taking them to her home? Will they be tortured in her house? Even after finding out that she is the thief, she has taken her out of the police station by telling a lie. Is not it a plan? Has not she thought of punishing the thief with her own hands?

All these things were swirling in Sabita's mind. The joy of escaping from the clutches of the police had vanished.

The car stopped in front of Sabitri Devi's house. Sabitri Devi got down from the car and asked them to get down too. Sabita saw that it was not a house but an institution, "Abandoned women's reform society." Many houses in a large area. Sabitri Devi lives in a small house out of it. All others are big long houses in which the helpless women who have been abandoned by their husbands, live. The organisation of Sabitri Devi is responsible for their maintenance.

First Sabitri Devi gave some food to the mother and son to eat. Then she took them to the office room and listened everything from Sabita. By this time, Sabita had overcome her fear and a bit of courage had come to her mind.

She asked in a slow and humble voice, "Madam ! why did you lie? We are the culprit. We deserve to be punished."

Sabitri Devi said, "if I had told the truth then what would have happened? I would have gotten my chain and you would have gone to jail. Your son would have been a destitute. Your son's future would have been ruined along with you. Now even if I lied, I got back my chain. But you two got a chance to reform your lives. If you want, you can stay here and work and your son can also go to school to study. This institution of mine is for helpless, abandoned women like you and their children.

Sabitri Devi was slightly disturbed. A look of sadness overshadowed her face.

What happened madam?

Sabitri Devi came to normal by Sabita's question and said "only a desolate woman can understand the miseries of another desolate woman. The truth is that we both are equally heart broken. That day, I heard from Kishor that your husband has left you. So I could know that what you are doing is due to extreme proverty and to satiate your own and your son's hunger. My story was that my family did not agree for the marriage with the person whom I loved because he was of lower caste. So I ran away and got married in a temple. He was a computer engineer, doing a good job. But what happened in the end? He went to Delhi on the plea of office work but did not return. Later, when I went to his office and inquired, I realised that he had actually gone abroad. I was qualified. So I looked for a job and luckily I got one. I saved money for the first ten years of my job. Then I started this organisation, which was my dream project. Because I had the experience. The pain and sufferings of the women deserted by their husbands had touched my heart. I had a weakness towards them. That's why I thought about such an organisation. Over the time, this organisation has become so big with government and private help.

Lying is a crime. But sometimes virtue can be earned by lying. Good works can be done. A lie that does not harm to anyone, but benefits others, is more glorious than the truth. The aroma of that lie spreads everywhere.

You know that Dharmaraj Yudhisthir had to lie in the Mahabharat war. On that day Dronacharya was the commander-in-Chief of the Kauraba army. He was invincible, irremediable. Hundreds and hundreds of Pandaba Soldiers were falling by the strike of his arrows. It was impossible to defeat him. But if not defeated, the Pandabas were sure to be vanquished. Meanwhile, on the advice of Shrikrishna, Bhima killed an elephant named Aswathama and word spread through out the battle field that Aswathama had died. The name of Drona's son was Aswathama. He could not believe that he was dead. To find out the truth, he brought his chariot in front of Yudhisthir's chariot and inquired about Aswathama. He firmly believed that Dharmaraj Yudhisthir would never lie.

But there Yudhisthir lied. Out of his mouth came,

"Aswathama hatha, Iti Norova Kunjarova." That means Aswathama died but it may be a human or an elephant. ? Iti Norova Kunjarova" he said so softly that Drona could not hear it. Grief-stricken by the death of his son, he gave up his weapons. And with that opportunity Draupadi's brother Dhrustadyumna killed him.

Here Yudhisthir lied for the preservation of religion, for the betterment of the country and for the benefit of the people.

Truth is not always good or lies are not always bad. As Shrikrishna said, "Sarba Bhuta hitam proktam, iti satya." It means that it is the only truth by speaking which all the beings are benefited.

Sabita heard all with amazement. After Sabitri Devi's discourse, she got up from her seat, held Sabitri Devi's feet and wept. Seeing his mother, Kishor also sat at Sabitri Devi's feet and cried. Sabitri Devi lovingly picked up both of them with her both hands and embraced them affectionately.

***

"There were lies we told to save ourselves, and then there were lies we told to rescue others. What counted more, the mistruth, or the greater good?" - Jodi Picoult

The Lost Time

Three days had elapsed since commencement of the hunger strike. Fasting unto death. Three days before when she came out of the jail, there were many people including some officials of voluntary organizations present there. The public prosecutor said, "you are now free, free of all guilt. You can go anywhere you want. You can do whatever you desire." She asked, "if I am free of any guilt, then for what crime was I kept in jail? Not a day or a half but twelve long years. I want justice now. From here I will go straight to the district collector's office. I will fast unto death there until I get justice." The public applauded her. Members of some voluntary organizations had announced to sit with her on the hunger strike. Damayanti had come to the district collector's office. The members of the voluntary organization who came with her built a small stage there in a short time and put a tent over it. They have got a chance. They have found a topic, to agitate for women's empowerment and against women's oppression. Seeing so much public support, even the police did not consider it proper to remove her. The hunger strike had started. The demand letter was submitted to the District Collector. There was only one sentence written on it, "Let me get justice. Give me my twelve years back."

It was already ten o' clock at night. By that time, the members of the organization had slept there on the carpet. Damayanti was sitting there leaning on a pillow. There was no sleep in her eyes. There was no hunger also. Her stomach was churning for the first one and two days. But there after it had no such sensation. An old song of Kishor Kumar was floating in the air from a distance from a radio or T.V., "Koi Lauta de mere bite hue din." Damayanti's mind was going back to the past, twelve years down the lane. She was remembering the events of twelve years ago.

Somehow their family life was going on smoothly. Her family consisted of her husband Duryodhan and two sons, five-year-old Somanath and three-year-old Rajanath. Duryodhan's two brothers Dushasan and Durjay lived separately from him. Both of them lived together. Only Duryodhan way isolated. Duryodhan's extreme anger was responsible for that. He was getting angry at the slightest pretext and used to beat his younger brothers. When the younger brothers grew up and got married, they could not tolerate it. There were arguments and quarrels. In the end everything was divided. A wall rose inside the yard, a fencing was done in the middle of the backyard and the cultivated lands were also divided in halves. But the younger brothers still complained that Duryodhan had made the wall by encroaching their two feet land. He had also taken bigger portion of land from the backyard. Duryodhan was a bit stronger. And everyday he used to drink some country liquor and make hoarse noises. He was emphatic , "I am the elder brother, as such I have taken a larger part of the property. No one can tell anything in this matter." Although the younger brothers could not say anything, their anger was bubbling inside. How long does it take to catch fire? All it requires is a little spark. With favourable winds, the spark can turn in to an inferno.

Every evening Duryodhan was returning home fully intoxicated. Damayanti also had a fight with him every day. This was a daily occurrence. Damayanti also got used to it. If something happenes every day, be it good or bad, one gets accustomed to it. Because of that, Damayanti was no longer so worried. But in order to control Duryodhan, she used to quarrel with him everyday. Twelve years ago, on that night, there was also an altercation between them. Duryadhan went to bed without eating anything. He was fully intoxicated and was lying like an unconscious person. Damayanti with her two sons slept in another room. She also locked the door from inside. So that if Duryodhan woke up from his sleep, he would not be able to come to this room.

Damayanti had no way of knowing the time at that point of night. But her sleep was broken by the sound of something. She opened the door and saw that the outside was fully illuminated. Soon she realized that a fire had broken out in Duryodhan's room. She went a little further and saw that Duryodhan's body was ablaze with fire. Duryodhan could not scream any more. Only was shaking a bit. Then that too also stopped. After absorving the initial shock, Damayanti screamed, "Fire, fire, please come running and save us." Along with it she was trying to put out the fire herself by bringing water in a bucket. Dushasan and Durjay came running but very late. Gradually the people of the village also gathered. All put out the fire together. But by then it was all over. Duryodhan had succumbed to death.

It was morning. But Damayanti knew that morning would never come again in her life. Only darkness and darkness. Even though the husband was a drunkard, still he was managing the house. But she did not have the time to think about that. Because, early in the morning the village chaukidar informed the matter in the nearest police station. The police officers had reached the spot. They started interrogating Damayanti, Dushsan, Durjaya and some other villagers. The police were convinced that it was a murder case and based on the testimony of all the witnesses they were suspicious of Damayanti. The police took Damayanti to the police station. Meanwhile, they released her for a few days for completion of Duryodhan's last rites. Then she was sent back to jail. Her trial was going on. The main witnesses against her were Dushasan and Durjay. From their statements, the police and the judge learned that Duryodhan used to drink alcohol everyday and that there were frequent squabbles between husband and wife. Damayanti poured kerosene on Duryodhan's body and set him on fire to escape from daily quarrels and beatings'. As a result he died. Match box and kerosene jerkin were recovered from the kitchen. The finger print of Damayanti was found on the match box. Taking all these evidences and circumstantial situations the judge was convinced that Damayanti was the murderer of Duryodhan and sentenced her to life imprisonment. Even though she shouted repeatedly that she was innocent but no one paid any heed to her words. Somanath and Rajanath were sent to an orphanage. Because the uncles refused to take their responsibilities.

Sometimes one gets punishment for doing nothing wrong. People are being victimized even though they are totally innocent. Though Damayanti was innocent, still she was sentenced to life imprisonment. She became known for committing mariticide even without doing anything.

Her husband died. She herself was in jail. It was not known whether she would come out of it during her life time or not. Her two children were in the orphanage. She had dreamt so many dreams about her two sons. She never thought that all the dreams of a person would be crushed in one go. She did not have enough resources to go to the high court against the lower court's decision. She felt total darkness around her. It was not within her power to solve it. So, surrendering herself completely in the hands of fate, she was only praying to God. Even, Draupadi prayed eagerly to Shrikrishna to protect her honour in the court of Kurus. Shrikrishna heard her prayer and saved her. Like that, can God not save a guiltless, innocent Damayanti?

While in jail, on the advice of a kind hearted, sympathetic Lawer, she filed a jail criminal appeal in the high court which was accepted by the honourable court. The government also provided a Lawer to fight on her behalf. After a long time, three days ago, the two judge bench pronounced their judgment. She is innocent. There is no strong evidence that she killed her husband. They also analysed that it is normal to have the house wife's finger prints on the match box in the kitchen. But her finger print was not detected on the kerosene Jerkin. There was a strong possibility that the murder was organized by some one else. And also opined that it was a miscarriage of justice to award life imprisonment to Damayanti.

The judges announced that there was a miscarriage of justice. They wrote it in one sentence but because of that her long twelve years had been wasted. As the saying goes, "happy days go on horses, sad days go on elephants." These twelve years seemed like twelve ages to her. Her life was ruined. Along with it the lives of her two sons were also destroyed. Can the long years of impression that their mother was the murderer of their father and therefore they have been stigmatized and humiliated in the society, ever be erased from their mind?

One thought was playing in her mind. She knew

that she was not guilty. The judges also declared that she was innocent. Then who could be the culprit? Surely Duryodhan is dead and he has been murdered. In that case, who is his murderer? What will happen to the police officer who investigated and found her guilty? Will the judge be punished for his wrong judgment for which she had spent twelve years in jail? Every one was silent about this. The police are silent, the courts are silent, the Law is silent, even the government is also silent. This silence has to be broken. Every body has to be enlightened that the Law states, "a hundred guilty may go scot free but one innocent should not be punished." Then why did Damayanti rotted twelve years in the prison without any guilt? Who can return the lost twelve years of her life? Who will answer all these questions?

Lord Ramachandra went to the forest for fourteen years to fulfill his father's promises. Fourteen years later he got his kingdom back. By the time he returned, Bharat had filled the royal treasury of Ayodhya completely. In the same way the Pandavas returned after twelve years of exile in the forest and one year of incognito life after losing in a dice game. Of course, they had to fight for their kingdom. But then they had Shrikrishana with them, with them also king Drupad's countless wealth and million and millions of army. They owned the war and got back their kingdom.

But what did she get after twelve years of imprisonment for no reason? So, she has to fight for her rights and for her properties. Yes! The hunger strike is a kind of silent war of this age.

The treasury bell in the distance struck four. Damayanti was trying to sleep for some time. Again there would be a gathering of people and journalists in the morning. Her body became very weak as she did not take any food for the last three days. She was drinking only a little water. She preferred to die rather than living a life like this. Where even her children hate her and do not want to come to her. Someone must have filled their mind with such poison that they did not come to see their mother even though she sent for them.

It was already morning. After finishing her daily routine works, Damayanti was seated on the stage. An official of the voluntary organization put a fresh garland around her neck. One of them had already started speaking. His speech was about women. He continued his speech, "The women are most tolerant. For that only women have been the epitome of sacrifice for ages. After the death of husband, the wife became sati (accompanying husband's dead body to the pyre and die with him). But when a wife dies, a husband never becomes a sati. They never performed self-immolation. After marriage the wife will wear glass bangles and vermilion for her husband. What a husband wears for his wife?"

The speech would have continued like this. Suddenly a lot of police personnel gathered there. Seeing so many police men, Damayanti thought, some thing is going to happen. She mentally strengthened herself. Whatever happens, she would not go back from her decision. She could see many vehicles coming. The entire atmosphere vibrated with the slogan of "Chief Minister – Zindabad." The police cleared a way amidst the crowd. The Chief Minister was coming towards her. Why was he coming? Before she could think anything, she saw the Chief Minister of the state standing before her.

Seeing him, Damayanti was trying to rise. But the Chief Minister did not let her get up. He held her hands and made her sit down again. Only then Damayanti could see her two sons. The Chief Minister's Personal Secretary was coming with them. Two sons embraced Damayanti. The tears of mother and sons brought tears to the eyes of everyone present there.

The Chief Minister said, "you see! You are of my daughter's age. Therefore, I am calling you as daughter. No one has the power to give you back your past twelve years. The time never turns back. So, I request you to forget those twelve years. Think that, those twelve years never came to your life. And our government has decided to compensate you for those twelve years. Twelve crore rupees will be given to you at the rate of one crore per year. Your old case file will be reopened and new investigation will be conducted and the real culprit will be punished. An inquiry will be started against the then officials. And the entire properties in your village which were occupied and enjoyed by the brothers of your husband will be returned to you. Apart from it, ten acres of land will be given to you by our government. This is all we can do. So, please break your fast by fulfilling the request of a person like your father."

Everyone could hear the words of the Chief Minister as the microphone was near him. The whole crowd applauded his decision. The officials of the voluntary organization also agreed to it and urged Damayanti to break the fast.

Damayanti was sitting impassively. She could not know what to do or not to do. How can she ignore the request of a person like her father and also the Chief Minister of the state. She will not get back her lost twelve years. So, is it not enough, what she has got now? She has got back her two sons who had turned away from her. She looked at him with tearful eyes. Some one gave a glass of fruit juice into the hands of the Chief Minister. He offered it to Damayanti. Damayanti took the glass with trembling hands. She broke her fast after sipping a little and touching the feet of the Chief Minister. As if the darkness had vanished from her eyes. Her body and mind were blooming with the arrival of a beautiful and golden morning. She embraced her two sons with affection who were standing next to her.

***

"There may be times when we are powerless to prevent injustice, but there must never be a time when we fail to protest."

- Elie Wiesel

The Sound Of Silence

There are some days in the life of every human being, which are remembered for ever. One such day is matric examination, the foundation level of children's lives. The more fortified it is, the stronger and brighter will be the child's future.

The result will be declared online at around 10 AM today. Of course, it will come to school immediately. It is already eight O'clock. Arati could not decide whether to go to school on not. This is the month of May. After a while the temperature will swell. She does not have a laptop or smart phone. So she will not be able to know the result as soon as it is declared. Of course some of her friends have promised to let her know the result. The closer the time to the result gets, the faster her heart beat increases. Not that she is apprehensive of any adverse result. After all she is known as a brilliant student. She is studying in this government school due to lack of money. But because she studies well, all the teachers and principal of the school have pinned a great hope on her. If she passes with good marks, the school's rank and fame will increase. For that only, she is scared. As her teachers love her and provide all kinds of help and support to her, can she fulfil their expectations? She took her bath, dressed and got ready to go to school. But at the last moment she sat down on a chair. Eventually some body will call and inform her, she thought.

Her mother, Minati, said, "eat something then go."

But Arati refused and said, "I will not eat anything until the result is out. I am also thinking not to go to the school, waiting for friend's phone call." She paid obeisance to God and again sat on the same chair.

It is already eleven O' clock. No body has telephoned. The result must have been announced by ten O'clock. Again half an hour passed. She became impatient. Without thinking anything, she switched on an odia news channel in her small T.V. It is reported that today at 10 O'clock in Cuttack Board Office the result of 10th class has been released by the education minster of the state. It is available online and also in every school. And what she heard next, she could not believe her ears. "Arati Mohapatra has stood first in the board examination of this year. She broke all the previous records at the state level."

When she turned around to tell her mother the good news, she saw her mother standing behind her; tears flowing from her both eye. She realised that these tears are not the tears of worry but of happiness and joy. She embraced her mother in a fit of passion. After a long time, mother and daughter's eyes were shinning with joy.

About an hour later, loud uproar was heard in front of her house. Immediately Arati came out and saw that the principal of the school, other teachers and some of her friends had gathered. She was very much worried. She could not invite them all to her small house. Before she could think anything, they took her out. Her friends carried her on their shoulders and danced. Some brought bouquets of flowers and some brought sweets. There was look of happiness on everyone's face. She got buried under the blessings of her teachers. This is the reflection of their love and affection.

After everyone left and the initial excitement

subsided, she felt an intense hunger. She had not eaten anything since morning. Minati quickly brought food for them. They both sat down to eat. Minati said, "Let us go to the market tomorrow. We will buy a good dress for you. I will also purchase a saree for me. Savitri puja is around the corner."

"No No, I do not need anything. You buy a good saree for you." Arati said.

What is the use of a good saree for me? I will buy one only to wear in the puja. There is no taste left in a burnt curry. However, as per my duty and as per our custom, I am observing this pooja every year. But for whom am I doing it, why am I doing it, I do not know.

Mother's moist voice disturbed Arati. She knows that her mother does this pooja every year. She never stops it. But plenty of sorrows remain buried in her mind. To change her mother's mind, she said, "first let us go today evening. I will eat chat and Golagopa to my hearts content. You will eat too. Your daughter has stood first in Odisa. It is a matter of great pride."

Minati smiled. She caressed the head of Arati with affection.

They slept earlier after taking dinner. Arati fell asleep as soon as she went to the bed. She was completely relaxed. She got the fruit of her labour of so many days. She was totally exhausted after talking on phone during the entire day. But Minati was not feeling sleepy. She was also very happy. Her years of penance have been successful and her vows have been fulfilled. But she was feeling an emptiness amidst so much joy. The events of the past few years danced in her mind's eye.

The dream of doing a job after completion of study remained as a dream. Her family tried for her marriage as soon as her M.A. examination was over. Her likes or dislikes were not thought of at all. Her marriage was solemnised with Bikas who was working in the Secretariat at Bhubaneswar. Bikas got a government quarter. Her marital life was going on happily. When Arati was born, their family life was completed. She was not able to know how and when the time passed by taking care of her daughter and doing household works.

Happy days may not always be there. Her happy life got eclipsed. Bikas must have fallen in some bad company. As a result, he started drinking a little bit of alcohol. At first Minati did not attach so much importance to these things. He was drinking very little at regular intervals. No one was harmed. No one had any problems. But her perception was wrong. The quantity of drinking continued to increase slowly. Alcohol is such an addiction, once one falls into its grip, it is very difficult to get rid of it. Bikas started drinking everyday. Most of the days he returned home fully drunk. Minati would wait for him without taking any food or drink. But he usually came and went straight to sleep. As the quantity of drinking increased so also the amount of money spent on drinking had increased. So he was unable to give enough money for the house expenses. Even it became difficult to purchase milk for their daughter. Minati tried hard to explain. But he refused to understand. One night there was fierce quarrel between the two. Minati got angry and said, "You give up alcohol or leave me."

Bikas also said in an angry voice, "I do not drink from anyone's father's money. I am earning and drinking from it. Whoever feels any inconvenience let her go." And in the heat of that argument, an inebriated Bikas slapped and abused Minati in filthy language.

Minati never expected that Bikas would raise his

hands on her. Her faith was severely hurt. The strength of endurance had exceeded the limit. For her, it appeared as if the rotation of the universe had stopped. Her heart was torn in to pieces. Without saying anything else, she quietly went and slept near her daughter. Tears were flowing from her eyes like the rains in the month of shraban. A violent storm arose in her mind. The golden dream of a sweet family she had seen, crumbled to dust. She thought that, Bikas could say so much because she had no income of her own. He must have thought that no matter what he said, Minati would be bound to stay there. But he must understand that Minati is a house wife, no... no... she is a home maker. Now the Supreme Court has said that the word "house wife" will not be used anymore. The term "home maker" will be used instead. Then what is the difference between these two words? House wife is the woman of the house where as home maker is the owner of the house. She is the master of the house. A woman wakes up early in the morning and does household works till late at night. At one point of time she is a house maid, cook, nurse, washer woman etc. Does she get paid for that? No., she does not think so. She does everything with a contented mind. She sacrifices her own happiness and comfort for the happiness of her family members. Such type of behaviour towards her is never acceptable. She has passed M.A. She can maintain herself by doing something. She or her daughter will not remain hungry on such a vast earth. Bikas was fully intoxicated and was lying on the bed. Minati kept her and Arati's necessary clothes and her gold ornaments and savings in a bag. She took her daughter and came out of the house before sunrise. She wrote a letter and kept it there, "Perhaps you do not need me anymore in your life. I am taking Arati with me. Do not let your shadow fall on her and do not try to come near me." After going some distance, she got up on a rickshaw and went to the house of one of her friends.

This happened ten years ago. Arati was only five years old. From that early age, the protective shadow of her father had disappeared. After staying for a few days at her friend's house, she searched a small house and left. Her friend requested her a lot to stay with her but dignified Minati did not stay. Meanwhile, she had contacted another friend whose father had a business of garment export. After telling everything to him, the gentleman promised to provide her sewing work. He was kind enough to provide her accommodation along with a sewing machine. Then her struggling life began.

A man gives pant and shirt clothes in the morning and takes the stitched garments in the evening. Minati is engaged in that work day and night. Arati's study was also going on along with it. By God's grace, Arati was studying well. Minati has never neglected her education.

In between, Minati's brother had come. Bikas had gone to him in search of her. Admitting his mistake, he wanted to take back Minati. But he was very much worried by not getting her there. Her brother explained to him that wherever she went, she would come back after her anger calms down and her mind became clear. He did not give her address.

After leaving the house, Minati told only to her brother everything and requested him not to tell anything to anyone and also not to divulge her address. However, her brother kept her request. But he tried to convince Minati and advised to go back home. But Minati was stubborn. She would not go there again. If once such an incident had happened, who could promise that it would not occur again. She will not allow all this to influence Arati. She can make her daughter a successful human being. This is our personal matter. No one should interfere in it.

Minati's brother did not mind such words told by her. He could understand that she was saying this in anger. But he said this much that "if you want you can go to the police. If you will lodge a complaint under domestic violence act, then he will come to his sense."

But Minati refused. She said, "what will happen if I complain to the police. A broken heart can not be joined. When one's golden dream has been crushed, what can be gained from the court and police. These will lead to mental turmoil and waste of time. All these can affect Arati too. Whatever God wills will happen." She stayed like this with her self-respect.

Today she is extremely happy on her daughter's success.

Arati was greeted with congratulations continuously. Meanwhile, a day way fixed, on which the Chief Minister of the state will felicitate the first ten students in the board examination in a famous theatre hall.

On the appointed day Minati and Arati went to that theatre hall. The organisers welcomed them and made them sit in the front row. The Chief Minister arrived on time and the program started. The Chief Minister himself honoured everyone. At the end of the function, it was Arati's turn. As usual the Chief Minister honoured her with a shawl and gifts and praised her. After the Chief Minister took his seat, the announcer requested Arati to speak something.

Arati stood behind the microphone. She looked around once and said after the opening address, "first of all, I apologize to everyone that I want to say something personal here. Some may not like it. But it is my request to listen with patience and please do not go away half way.

May be some rays of light can be shed in the dark sky of an unfortunate family. Today is a happy day for me.

My mother contributed a lot for my success. Her love, inspiration, efforts have brought me to this place. It has been ten years since she sacrificed all her happiness only for me. Like Lord Shiva, she drank all the poisons and showered nectar on me. I am proud of her. But in all this, a great deficiency has saddened me. Today only my mother is with me. My father exists, again does not exist. They have been staying separately for ten long years because of only one mistake. I do not hesitate to say here that my father's excessive drinking was the root cause of their misunderstandings. After drinking, he was always out or his senses and misbehaved with my mother. My mother was totally upset and left the house with me. She provided me good education with her tireless efforts. Father also stayed alike with anger and stubbornness. I will say only this much that the reason for which our house is ruined, that should not occur in anyone's life. But despite staying apart for so many years, neither of them ever tried to get a divorce. My mother observes Savitri puja every year with full devotion. I can understand that their hearts are full of love and affection for each other. My father visited me once in the school and said that he was not coming to visit me as my mother   had denied it. He gave up alcohol altogether. The river, which was flowing smoothly, suddenly turned into two streams with the obstruction of a huge rock and flowed on either side of the rock. One river is devided into two streams but the destination is the same, i.e. to join the sea. Then, can not the two streams become one river again before joining the sea?

I strongly believe my father is present here among the spectators. Because he will be unable to supress the desire to heartfully enjoy his daughter's success. I request, father ! if you really love your daughter, forget all your anger, arrogance and come to this stage. I am also appealing my mother to come here. I want the blessings of you both together and from here we, the three of us, will go to our home and start a happy new chapter as a family. And if you do not come, then I will not continue my study further. I will engage myself in swing the clothes as my mother. I will wait for two minutes only. Because many great persons and the Chief Minister have come. I do not want to waste their precious time.

Arati became silent. A stunning silence filled the entire theatre hall. Even if a leaf falls, its sound can be heard. Minati slowly came and stood on the stage. Her inner feelings were not visible from her face. She was very calm. Everyone was very much anxious, "will Arati's father really come?" Suddenly a gentle man wearing a hat got up from a back seat and slowly walked towards the stage. Spontaneously Arati uttered, Ba… ba… Everyone could here it as the mike was in front of her. As soon as the gentleman stood on the dais, Minati bent down and touched his feet. Forgetting the place, the time and the people, the gentleman picked up Minati with both hands and embraced her. As if the time stood still for both of them. There was no word in either's mouth. Both were silent. But silence also had a voice. Only those who understand it can realise.

Arati touched the feet of both. The theatre hall shook with applause. They all stood up and started leaving.

***

"Silence is the language of God, it is also the language of the heart." - Sivananda

Black Eagle Books

www.blackeaglebooks.org
info@blackeaglebooks.org

Black Eagle Books, an independent publisher, was founded
as a nonprofit organization in April, 2019. It is our mission
to connect and engage the Indian diaspora and the world at
large with the best of works of world literature published on
a collaborative platform, with special emphasis on
foregrounding Contemporary Classics and New Writing.

www.ingramcontent.com/pod-product-compliance
Lightning Source LLC
Chambersburg PA
CBHW050324110726
47899CB00007B/2356